ONE HUNDRED CHRISTMAS KISSES

AN ASPEN COVE SMALL TOWN ROMANCE

KELLY COLLINS

BOOK NOOK PRESS

To every reader who has invested their time reading my work. Thank you!
It takes more than a great story to create a novel or in this case a novella. The author comes up with an idea and runs with it, but without moral support, the talent of a graphic designer, an editor, proofreaders, publicist, PA and a formatter, it's just words on paper.
Thank you for loving Aspen Cove!

CHAPTER ONE

Evan Barkman was an asshole and an awful kisser. He was also Charlie's boss, which made kissing him under the mistletoe the biggest mistake she ever made. It's why she didn't mix Christmas parties with alcohol. That was three days ago and she hadn't spoken to him since. Well, she'd spoken to him because he was her boss, but their words were purely professional. They discussed puppies, bowel obstructions, and fleas.

"If I asked you to stay would you? I invited you on my trip," Evan said.

While he locked up the pharmaceuticals, she walked around the operating table to toss the soiled linens into the laundry bag. They'd just removed a balloon from a beagle's lower intestine and this would be the last laundry pickup before the holidays.

"No, I told you I'm going to Aspen Cove to visit family." She had been on the fence about going home, but Evan's badgering made the unpleasant thought of seeing her father more palatable. It had been ten years since they were together in the same room. That room had been the funeral home in Copper Creek. They closed her mother's casket and she closed that chapter on her life. After eight years of schooling and two years working for an idiot, Charlie was ready to take a step back and re-evaluate everything. Changes needed to be made.

Evan walked around the table toward her, and she moved to the other side to avoid him.

"Why are you running from me?"

"I'm not running." She made sure to keep at least a three-foot barrier between them. The damn man had long arms. "I told you the kiss was a mistake. It was too many spiced eggnogs mixed with poor judgment."

The fact that he'd maneuvered her under the mistletoe was another story altogether. He'd been getting friendly over the last few months. Each time he passed her in the clinic, he found a reason to touch her. What started out as a graze of the hands across her back turned into a pat on the bottom or a brush of his arm across her breast. He had a sea of space to walk around, but he always chose the exact place she stood to crowd her.

"I don't think it was a mistake. The kiss was perfect." He made it around the stainless steel table before she could outmaneuver him. His hands gripped her shoulders and his lips covered her mouth. Cover was exactly right. Evan Barkman had a mouth the size of the Grand Canyon. It dripped saliva like Niagara Falls.

She pushed at his chest, but he held his position. He pulled back and said, "We're perfect for each other, Charlie. It's a match made in heaven."

She knew that her next move would end everything, including her job. "We're not a match. You're a veterinarian and should know you can't mate a water buffalo with a feline and come out with something good."

"This could be good." He pressed himself against her.

She positioned her knee for impact. When it connected to his groin, everything changed. His hands left her shoulders and dropped to his crotch. He stumbled back. "Why would you do that?" His voice had the pitch of a six-year-old girl.

"Because you're an asshole, and I quit." Charlie took off her lab coat and tossed it onto the table, walking out of Barkman's Veterinary Clinic. Her job there had lasted two years. At least it would be a solid reference. She'd make sure to remind Mr. Barkman what a stellar veterinarian she was when she called to pick up her final paycheck and threaten to sue him for sexual harassment.

She stomped straight to her SUV and climbed inside. Her head fell to the steering wheel and she cried. Her tears flowed freely. Wasn't it time to let all the anguish go? When she finished drying her cheeks with the hem of her pink scrub shirt, she started her car and took off toward home.

As if the universe was pushing her forward, Agatha Guild's number popped up on her cell. She transferred the call to bluetooth.

"Hey, Agatha, how are you?"

"I'm finer than frog hair split seven ways, sweetheart. Just checking to see if you've decided to come for a visit?"

Agatha was her father's new girlfriend and Charlie wasn't sure how to feel about the woman who had stepped in to replace her mother. On one hand, she was grateful that her father wasn't alone. Then again, she didn't know how her mother could have been replaced. She had to give credit to the woman for being persistent in her quest to get Charlie Parker back to Aspen Cove. She'd called twice a week for the last six months.

"I'm in the car. I have to stop by my apartment and pick up my bag, and then I'll be on my way. Please don't tell my dad. I'd like it to be a surprise." What she really meant was she didn't want him to be disappointed if she got halfway and turned around because she lost her nerve.

"My lips are sealed. I can't wait to meet you in person, Charlie. I've heard so much about you from your father that I almost feel like I know you already."

"You do know me, somewhat. You've been like a dog with a bone trying to get me there with your calls."

"There is that." Agatha laughed. It was a soft trill of a sound that floated through the line.

Charlie knew without a doubt that she'd like her. That made her guilt even worse.

"I'm staying at the bed and breakfast. I'll call you in the morning when I get up." She'd made the reservation last week. It broke her heart that Bea no longer owned the place, but people got old and change was inevitable. For those reasons alone, it was time to mend fences with her dad. He was no spring chicken and after he got injured in a fire, which was why Agatha called in the first place, she'd given their situation a great deal of thought.

"Drive safely, Charlie. There's a storm moving in."

Great. "No problem. I drive in the snow all the time." Not exactly a lie, but the inches they got in Kansas City would never compare to the feet they got in Colorado.

She hung up the phone and zipped by her apartment to change, get her suitcase, and pick up her computer. She'd need it since she'd have to look for a new job. The weather channel put a fire under her bottom. If she hurried, she might be able to beat the storm coming in from Albuquerque. She remembered all too well how the storms from the south brought too much moisture with them.

She grabbed a box of Little Debbie Cosmic Brownies and headed out. If she was lucky, she'd make the near seven hundred mile trip by midnight. Maybe quitting her job wasn't such a bad thing. It got her finished before noon. Then again, they were closing for the holidays, regardless. Thankfully, Dr. Barkman took two weeks off each year at Christmas to visit his mother in Florida.

Charlie wondered if she'd still get her Christmas bonus. While she wasn't going to be homeless tomorrow, she would need to find a tenable situation soon.

Five hours into the drive, the flakes began to fall. She stopped for gas and pressed onward.

Had it really been ten years since she'd seen him? When her mother died she couldn't forgive her father for not saving her. He was like a god in that region. People drove for miles to see Doctor Paul Parker because he always had the answers.

Her anger was the immature thought process of an eighteen-year-old girl who'd lost her mom. At fifty-eight, Phyllis Parker had been healthy as a horse. Not that all horses were healthy, but her mother had never had a health problem until the stroke, which was caused by a brain aneurism. How many people had her father saved and yet he couldn't save his wife?

The guilt of her decision to pack up and go to college and never look back was what had kept her away. How could she make up for ten years of abandonment? She couldn't.

The windshield wipers picked up their pace as the snow fell heavy and thick on the glass. Like an old lady, Charlie sat forward with her chin nearing the top of the steering wheel. She slowed to a sloth's pace. She'd just made it past Denver when a red Mustang whizzed past her.

"Idiot," she said aloud. "Even I know a front wheel drive won't make it through the pass."

It seemed that whoever was in that car was trying to race the storm that was already on top of them. Or he was the idiot of her initial thoughts. She said a silent prayer for the person because she wished no harm on anyone.

After a quick stop for a bathroom break and a coffee, she entered the pass that would take her through the winding mountainside. She halfway considered turning back but didn't because she was almost there. Almost being a loose term meaning she had less miles to go than she'd already traveled. While the treacherous terrain of snowy, icy roads and idiot drivers were in front of her, there was nothing left behind her. She wondered if somewhere deep inside she'd created a situation where the only path left was forward.

She considered the future and what it might bring. At this point there were three things Charlie needed more than anything in the world. She needed a new job. She needed her father. She needed to forgive herself because, even though she'd blamed her father all those years ago, she truly felt responsible for her mother's death. They'd fought that morning over where she'd go to college. Charlie wanted to attend college out of state. She wanted to experience life outside of a small town. Her mother had begged her to stay. That was part of the problem with being the only child of a couple who'd struggled to get pregnant. All their hopes and dreams landed on Charlie's shoulders and it was a weight too heavy to bear.

She could still see her mother's red face in her memory. And her last words would haunt her for life. She'd told Charlie that she'd just die if she was so far away. While realistically, Charlie knew it was a figure of speech, not more than an hour after their argument, Phyllis Parker was dead.

That was the minute everything changed. She knew that she could never be anyone's everything. To do so put her heart at risk and she'd never survive anything so heartbreaking as losing someone else she loved. It was why she was on the fence about making up with her father. What if just as she entered his life again, he exited hers? She'd never survive.

Lately, she'd been hearing the whispers of her mother's voice in her memory. Phyllis Parker was like a white, female Gandhi with all her quips and quotes. Charlie once asked her mother about finding love and was told that you don't find love, it finds you.

She'd been waiting for years for it to find her. One thing she knew for certain was it didn't come dressed in a lab coat and give sloppy kisses. If that were her only chance at love then she'd start filling her apartment with cats.

CHAPTER TWO

"You ready, buddy?" Trig Whatley put a pillow on the front bucket seat of his Mustang and hefted his dog into place. Clovis was simply too fat to make the leap from the parking lot into the car. The basset hound was downright obese. While he was supposed to be Trig's emotional support dog, it would appear that Clovis needed support too. He had a mean Milk Bone habit. Add to that the Beggin' Strips addiction and he was in need of a twelve-step program. The dog settled into the pillow, lowered his muzzle and closed his eyes.

Trig looked over his shoulder to the water. He would miss living at the beach. He'd done a lot of healing and a lot of hurting here. It was on the strand, the wide cement walkway where he trained for the Rock and Roll Marathon. He looked at the waves and recalled the first time he'd body boarded after the accident. Terrified the salt water would irritate his already unhappy stump, he put off going into the water for months, but there were too many string bikinis diving into the surf to ignore. In the water, he appeared to be just like everyone else. It was when he got on land that the differences were noted.

The men looked at him like he was less than them and the women stared at him with pity.

That was where the hurt began. He could overcome the physical pain of losing his left leg below the knee, but the emotional pain was brutal. He was no less of a man than the day his Humvee was destroyed by an IED.

He gave the beach one last look and backed out of the parking lot. He'd sublet his studio apartment to a guy from his gym. Trig had no idea where this visit would lead but he hoped it would give him some clarity. With a permanent disability check, he wasn't hurting for cash but he was hurting. All Trig wanted was to find a place where he felt normal, and to find a woman who would look at him and know that missing a leg didn't make him less in any way.

"And we're off."

Clovis lifted his head.

"You, my friend, need more exercise." He took the last Beggin' Strip from the bag he had shoved into the cup holder and gave it to the dog. "This is the last one. We are cutting back on shit that isn't good for us. I'm giving up feeling sorry for myself, and you're giving up empty calories and all-day naps."

The dog chewed on the treat slowly, like he was savoring the snack because it was his last. They pulled into the parking lot of a grocery store to get supplies for the trip.

"You want to come with me or stay in the car?"

Clovis looked at him, gave him a shake of his tail and went back to sleep.

"Suit yourself, but you're getting carrot sticks from here on out."

Trig wondered if Clovis was depressed. He'd watched Trig pack up their belongings. He'd gone with him to storage on several occasions. Over the last few weeks, they'd been living out of boxes while Trig decided where to go on their first adventure. When a call came from his army buddy Bowie telling him he should visit, Trig didn't hesitate to say yes.

He got out of the car and pulled his pant

leg over his prosthetic. He had several now. The first one he got looked like a shoe on a stick. The second one was modeled after his good leg minus the scarring from shrapnel. The third was his favorite. The blade runner was the most comfortable because it was designed for running. It was like walking on a springy cloud. It also got him through the marathon. While he didn't come in first, he did pass the finish line before many able-bodied racers. Today he wore the shoe on a stick because it had a loose fit and felt more comfortable on long trips.

He walked through the store, throwing protein bars, bags of nuts and fruit in his cart. He got the baby carrots for Clovis and a case of water for them both.

"Excuse me." A sweet voice came from the end of the aisle. "Can you help me reach something?"

He turned to see a hot redhead stepping onto the bottom shelf in front of her. "Wait, I'll get it."

She giggled and blushed as he walked over. This was how it always started—nice flirtatious conversation.

"What flavor were you reaching for?" Why the stockers put things so high was beyond him. He'd found it frustrating to accomplish anything when he'd been wheelchair bound. Hard to believe that was only two years ago.

"I really like the peach tea." She pointed to the top of a beverage display. "But that's the only one left and I can't reach it."

"No problem." He lifted on his right leg and caught the box by his fingertips. Trig yanked it forward, not realizing he'd loosened the row below it. Without warning, the entire display toppled over with him tumbling with it. Before he knew it, he was on his back surrounded by a sea of Snapple. In his hands, raised above his head, was the box he'd reached for.

"Success." He handed the woman the box and struggled to his feet.

"Oh my God, you're soaked." She pulled the roll of paper towels from her cart and went straight to dabbing him dry. He tried to move out of her reach, but she followed his retreat.

"I'm fine. You don't have to—"

She wrapped her hands around his prosthetic leg, trying to dry his pants, then stopped. Her eyes lifted to his face. "Oh shit, you're handicapped."

Once again, he was no longer just a man helping out a woman. He moved back and gave her a look he knew frightened her by the way she scurried away from him.

"No, I'm handy. I was the one who got your tea. Let's leave it at that."

She let her chin drop and her shoulders round. "I'm sorry. You're right. Thank you for your help."

Trip nodded and walked away in his tea-soaked pants. He wondered why it felt like he was the one who had to educate the world.

He threw a few more items into his cart and made his way to the checkout.

"Let me get your groceries," the woman he'd helped said from behind him.

He bristled at the offer. While he was sure it was meant as a kind gesture, it still bothered him.

"Why?" He loaded his items onto the belt.

"It's the least I can do for your help."

"Would you have bought the groceries for a different person who helped or is it because I have one leg?" He pushed the issue because he was tired of feeling different. The only way to stop that would be to make people realize how differently they treated him.

She looked down at his left foot. The hem of his khaki pants appeared brown.

"You're right. I probably would have said thank you and moved on."

"So do it."

She bit her lip. When it popped free she asked, "Do what?"

Trig smiled. "Say thank you and move on."

She nodded. "Thank you." She gave him a last look before she stepped away and continued her shopping.

The cashier told him his total and added, "You were amazing."

Trig looked up to see an older woman smile. "Why?"

"Because you taught her something she'll never forget." She leaned over the counter and looked at his wet pants. "War injury or something else?"

"IED," he said like it was everyday conversation. "Amputation below the knee."

She nodded. "My son lost his arm. Hates the sad looks and pity parties." She processed his payment and bagged up his purchases. "Thank you for your service and your sacrifice. Don't forget, you're more of a man now than you ever were."

Trig picked up his bags and made his way back to the Mustang. If that cashier hadn't been nearing sixty, he would have fallen in love with her.

He tossed the bags into the back seat and opened the trunk to get a change of clothes. In five minutes, he and Clovis were back on the road.

Many hours later, his phone rang. He knew by the ringtone it was Bowie. He was the only one linked to "The Army Goes Rolling Along."

"What's up, Sarge?"

"Stop with the Sarge shit," Bowie said. "I no longer outrank you."

Trig laughed. "Dude, you saved my life. You'll always outrank me." The nightmares had finally passed, but he still had dreams of Sergeant Bishop telling him he'd be okay as he tightened the tourniquet around his leg. All he could see was Bowie's blood soaking the desert sand beneath them. He'd seen to Trig's injuries before his own. He'd always been a good leader, but that day was a testament to Bowie's character. He'd taken care of his men first.

"Where are you at?"

"I'm about six hours from Denver, then three from you, I guess. There's been a storm chasing my ass all the way from Albuquerque, but I've been able to outrun it."

"You're driving all the way through in one shot?"

"If I stop I might not make it there. I'm in the Mustang."

"You got chains?"

"No, but I've got caffeine and desire. That's got to count for something."

Bowie laughed. "Yep, lack of brains. You'll never make it over the pass."

"I'll get there." He gave Clovis a quick glance. "Worst case, I'll have Clovis hooked up to sled and he can drag my tired ass there."

"He still living on bacon and biscuits?"

"Nope, he's transitioned to carrot sticks and grain-free kibble." Trig reached over to pet Clovis, who was happily lying on his back, all four paws sticking up toward the soft top of his car.

"Be safe. Call me if you get stuck. I'll come and get you."

"Will do." He hung up and popped the top on another can of Jolt. As he drove through the eastern part of Colorado stopping off at Fort Carson to quickly see a buddy, the clouds thickened and the flakes grew larger. Things were looking ugly outside.

As he left Denver and entered the mountains, he knew he had a fifty-fifty shot of getting to Aspen Cove by nightfall. He whizzed past a white Jeep going no more than thirty miles an hour and hoped he could beat the storm all the way there. Those hopes were dashed when he reached the turnoff to take him between Mount Meeker and Longs Peak. His car fishtailed and he found himself plunged into a snow bank on the side of the road where no amount of spinning his wheels would unstick him.

Clovis started to whine, which meant he needed a potty break. Trig opened the door and Clovis took off toward the edge of the woods. Trig ran after him but the snow got deeper and deeper.

"Clovis, get over here," Trig yelled. His voice echoed in the eerie silence of the snowfall. He searched the edge of the tree line for the sausage-shaped dog. He heard a yelp before the dog hopped and sunk and hopped and sunk into the snow all the way back.

Trig swept him up into his arms. "You silly boy. You could have been buried in that mess." He placed Clovis back on the front seat pillow.

After a few swipes of his paws to his eyes, Clovis was back asleep and Trig pulled out his phone to call for help. Help he'd never reach without a signal, which he didn't have. His best hope now was for someone as stupid as him to be traveling in the weather to pass him by.

He eyed the road for over an hour while the snow built up on his car. No one was traveling in this mess. In another hour, his red Mustang would be covered in white and no one would see him. In the distance, he thought he saw the glow of headlights.

"Come on, Clovis, you're our ticket to a ride." Trig was smart enough to know that no one would stop for a single man, but add in a dog and he'd get a ride for sure. Make it a basset hound with those long floppy ears and eyes that pleaded his case, and they'd be in Aspen Cove in no time.

He stood by the side of the road and waved his arms as the car approached slowly. Clovis did his part by shivering and looking pathetic.

CHAPTER THREE

Charlie couldn't believe her eyes. Standing on the side of the road dressed in jeans and a T-shirt was a man waving his arms. Next to him was a shivering blob of fur. Normally she'd never stop for a stranger, but that dog looked like it would turn into a pupcicle at any minute.

She pulled onto the soft shoulder as the anger boiled inside her. She didn't give a damn if the man froze to death. He had opposable thumbs and that made him capable of taking care of himself, but that poor little sad-eyed hound. She couldn't turn her back on him.

She killed the engine and looked around for a weapon. A girl could never be too safe. Too bad she hadn't thought about that before she left

Kansas City. All she had was a can of soda, a candy bar, and a half-empty box of cosmic brownies. She'd never heard of death by Snickers or bludgeoning by brownies, so she picked up the can and opened her door. Worst scenario she could club the man until the carbonation exploded from the can and then her best hope was to drown him. She'd never heard of a person drowning in a can of soda before, so she went back to the bludgeoning idea.

As she rounded the Jeep, her heart raced, which only added to her anger and angst. Her common sense left her as she pocketed her soda can and raced to the poor dog.

"Are you insane?" She pulled her phone from her pocket, which had no signal but showed the last temperature reading as eighteen degrees. "He's going to get frostbite."

Charlie ignored the man and swept the dog into her arms. "Oh, sweetheart, are you okay?" She lifted his paws one by one and inspected the pads for damage. "You are so lucky."

"Hello." The man's low gravelly voice sounded behind her. "Thanks for stopping."

Charlie had nearly forgotten about him in her attempt to rescue the dog. "How could I not? It's basically animal abuse."

The man stepped in front of her and held

out his arms for the dog. "Does Clovis look mistreated to you?"

She had to admit that the animal didn't appear to be in danger. In fact, when she felt his pads, they were soft and pliable, which meant the pup couldn't have been outside for long.

"He's overweight, and that in and of itself could be considered animal cruelty."

He took the dog from her arms. "We're working on that, aren't we, boy?"

He pressed his face into the dog's fur and nuzzled him, which gave Charlie a warm buzz that floated through her veins despite the freezing temperature and falling snow.

She looked past him to the Mustang. "Not really a winter car." She lifted her eyes and waited for him to argue, but he didn't.

"Nope. I thought I could beat the storm, but it looks like it beat me. I'll have to call a tow when I get someplace that has reception." He brushed the snow that settled on his head. "Any way you can give us a lift to the next town?"

She laughed. "There's not much between here and Copper Creek. A few small towns is all, but sure, I'll give you a lift."

He looked between her Jeep and his car. "Do you have room for a few of my things?"

She wondered if she was making a mistake,

but she realized how silly that thought was. No man with a basset hound and a sports car came to the mountains to murder her.

"Grab whatever you want to take. The back seat is empty and there's only a suitcase in rear storage. What's your name, by the way?"

He smiled. "Thought you'd never ask." He hefted the dog into one arm and offered his hand to shake. "I'm Trig Whatley."

She shook his hand. "I'm Charlie Parker."

He lifted a brow the way most people did when she said her name. "Charlie?"

She nodded. "Short for Charlotte, but I liked bugs better than bows growing up so my mom and dad called me Charlie. Let me hold the beast while you get your things."

Trig put Clovis in her arms and headed to his car. The first thing he pulled out was a pillow and bag of mini-carrots. He walked to her Jeep and got the dog settled before he went back for anything else. Another flush of warmth washed through her.

Next, he pulled out a few grocery bags. Lastly, he grabbed an army-green duffel from the trunk. He locked up the car and climbed into the passenger seat, and they were off.

"Where's your final destination?" she asked.

He looked out the window. "I don't know

where I'll land in the end, but I was on my way to visit an old army buddy named Bowie."

Charlie's head whipped toward him at the mention of Bowie. "Bowie Bishop?" She had been a half-dozen years behind him in school but she remembered the Bishop boys well.

Trig turned his body toward her. He seemed to get his left leg tangled, and had to adjust his position. "You know him?"

"Yep, I grew up in Aspen Cove. Hard to believe he's still there." She had no idea who was around and who wasn't. It wasn't as if she'd kept in touch with anyone since her abrupt exodus.

"Is that where you're going—to Aspen Cove?" he asked. A look of joy eased the lines in Trig's forehead.

"Yep, looks like you'll get to hitch a ride all the way there." She moved forward so she could see the road in front of her.

"Are you going to drive twenty miles an hour the whole way?"

She shot him a quick dirty glance. "Do you want to get there alive? If you hadn't noticed, it's dropping snow at a rate of a few inches per hour. I'm not the one stuck in a snow bank."

"Alive sounds good, but getting there before we turn gray sounds appealing too."

"Should I pull over and let you out? I'm

happy to deliver Clovis to wherever you're staying."

"Nope, I'll shut up and be grateful. Thank you."

"Look at you...cute and smart." She wanted to bury herself in the snow when the word cute came out unintended, but it was the truth. Trig Whatley was a damn fine-looking man. "Not too smart because you were standing outside in freezing temperatures in a T-shirt. Don't you have a jacket?"

"I do but it was in my bag and I didn't want to stop to get it. I saw your lights and I had to decide if I wanted a ride or wanted to stay warm. I chose to play off your sympathies first. If you had passed me, I would have dug my jacket out. But you didn't. You stopped because I looked smart and cute."

Charlie dared a glance at the man, who wore a smug expression.

"I stopped for the dog."

Trig looked back at his dog and reached out to pet his head. "Thanks for being so pathetic looking. She stopped for you."

"It's a work hazard. I'm a veterinarian. I can't turn away from fur, feathers, or fins. What about you? Still in the army?"

"No, I gave that up a few years ago. The

green camouflage didn't go well with my skin tone."

She giggled. She liked that he could joke. So many men were too serious.

"I'm kind of figuring out what I want to do next. I thought maybe I could be the next dog whisperer. The trick to getting them to behave is in the bacon."

"No wonder he's fat."

"Hey, don't say that too loud. He's quite sensitive about his figure."

At the mention of bacon, Charlie's stomach growled. She hadn't eaten much today trying to beat the storm. She reached for the Snickers. "You want half?"

"Save that for dessert. I've got you covered." Trig reached into her back seat and fumbled around in the bags he'd set there. He turned back around with his hands full. "I've got protein bars for energy, fruit for taste, nuts because...well, they're just good." He lifted the package of jerky in the air. "I brought the beef."

Charlie couldn't believe where her mind went. He said jerky and she thought meat stick. That made her think of *his* meat stick and her face heated. Thankfully, with the storm, the interior of the car had taken on a gray color she hoped would hide her blush.

She'd checked the man out the whole time he was transferring his belongings to her car. He was tall, stocky, and well-muscled, if the way his damp T-shirt clung to his chest was an indicator. His legs were long and lean with jeans that hugged powerful thighs. He moved with purpose like every step was planned in advance.

"You want a piece?"

She'd lost track of the conversation. How could she think when the man was offering her his meat? She felt him press a piece to her lips and she opened her mouth. "Thanks," she said with a giggle. Never had a man gotten her to open her mouth and take what he offered so easily.

One thing was certain—Trig Whatley was going to be a distraction for her. It was a good thing that she'd be able to drop him off at the Bishops' and forget about him.

She wound her way through the mountain pass. They sat in companionable silence while she ate his jerky, his nuts, and his fruit. She offered him half of her Snickers.

"I imagine it would be rude to not taste what you're so freely offering." His voice had that slow, sexy sound that made it seem like she had offered more than a half of a candy bar.

When he bit into his half of one of the best

things known to man outside of cosmic brownies and good sex, he moaned with satisfaction. Charlie wondered if a person could orgasm from chocolate. Many women have said that chocolate is better than sex. She hadn't indulged in enough of either lately to make a solid call.

"Five more minutes and we'll be there. Should I drop you off at the Bishops' house?"

He glanced back at Clovis. "Nope. I think I'll get him settled into the bed and breakfast and then walk over. Bowie said he lived next door."

She couldn't believe what she heard. "You're staying at B's?"

"Yep, we weren't sure how the dogs would get along, and now that Bowie has a wife and a little girl, I don't want to upset their routine. He told me his brother's fiancée owns the bed and breakfast."

"Great." She got her heartbeat to slow down enough so she wouldn't faint. "Looks like we'll be staying at the same place."

"Really?" He sounded almost excited. "What are the chances that I get stuck and then rescued by a woman heading to the same town, and the same place I am?"

She had no real answer. "Wild, right?"

Charlie pulled through town at a snail's pace. It wasn't because of the snow on the ground but because she wanted to take it all in. On the edge of town stood a brand new Firehouse. She wondered how the tiny little town afforded it. As she passed the shops, she noted that nothing much had changed. All the players remained the same except the Dry Goods Store was back in business, as was Kathy's Beauty Shop, even though it was no longer called Kathy's, but Cove Cuts.

As she drove down Main Street, she saw the sign of her father's clinic was turned off. Her eyes went straight to where the tailor shop used to be. That should have been her vet clinic. It had always been the plan until her mother died. She let out a sigh and a silent wish for something good to come from this visit.

CHAPTER FOUR

Trig was happy to exit the Jeep and stretch his leg. He often found himself restless when sitting. Anxious when he was a passenger in a car. Downright terrified when the driver drove seventeen miles an hour.

He had to get it out of his head that he wasn't in the desert and that IEDs weren't planted around every turn, but fear was a beast he hadn't been able to tame. He moved through life fast so nothing could catch him.

The front door opened and a miniature Bowie walked onto the porch. "You must be Cannon," Trig said.

He looked from Trig to Charlie. "Bowie said you had a dog, not a woman." He stared at Charlie, who was still in the SUV. "If he was calling her a dog, I'd say you owe him an ass-kicking."

He glanced at the woman in the front seat. She was definitely not a dog, and while she wasn't Beach Barbie pretty, she was beautiful in a wholesome girl-next-door way. "We're not together."

Charlie killed the engine and stepped out of the Jeep.

"You drove together, but you're not together?" Cannon asked as he took a few steps forward. "Charlie? Is that you?"

"Cannon Bishop, you've changed." She raced to him and threw her arms around his waist for a big hug.

"Holy hell, girl." He stood back and took her in. "You grew up."

A tiny little redhead came to stand next to Cannon. She looked at the woman standing in front of him. "You have to be Charlie. You favor your father for sure."

Charlie's hands rose to her face. "You think so?"

"Yep, same kind eyes but a lot less wrinkles." She offered Charlie her hand. "I'm Sage Nichols. I'm the new owner of B's Bed and Breakfast, and I also work at your father's clinic." She elbowed Cannon in the side. "You already know this guy." She looked past them to Trig. "Did you bring a roommate?"

Charlie looked at him and blushed. "No, we're not together." She rolled her pretty blue eyes. "I mean, we drove the last leg of the trip together because this guy"—she pointed to him— "thought he could make it through the pass in a Mustang—convertible no less."

"That makes you Trig," Cannon said. "Where's your dog?"

Trig opened the back door and helped Clovis to the ground. He went to the nearest tree and lifted his leg.

"Sorry about that," Trig said.

Out of the front door came a big ball of fur. Trig watched the dog with three legs race to Clovis. The tri-pod animal fascinated him. The two dogs circled each other. It was as if all they needed was a sniff to know they belonged together. Too bad humans weren't so easy.

"That's Otis."

"How'd he lose his leg?" Charlie asked.

Sage shook her head. "I was told he got hit by a car, but I don't really know. I adopted him."

"That was a big commitment to take on his long-term medical costs."

Sage shrugged. "He doesn't seem to mind that he's missing a leg. We don't care either."

Right then, Trig knew he was going to enjoy this holiday. Surely the three-legged dog was a sign.

"Let me help you with your things." Cannon turned to Trig. "I know Bowie is dying to see you."

Trig went to get Clovis, who gave him a look that said leave-me-be as he trotted behind Otis.

Sage helped Charlie with her bag while Cannon threw Trig's duffel over his shoulder and walked inside the house. Trig and Charlie were led to the end of a hallway where they were given side-by-side rooms.

"Thanks for the ride," Trig said before he walked inside his space.

"It was nice to not have to make the trip alone. I liked your company."

"You did?"

"Yes, I did."

Cannon stepped out of Trig's room after putting his duffel inside and stared at the two guests. "Are you sure you two aren't together-together?"

Charlie blushed. "Of course not."

"All right." He shrugged and walked down the hallway. "Get yourselves settled." He pointed at Trig. "I'll tell my brother you'll be over in a few."

Trig lifted his chin in acknowledgement, but his eyes never left Charlie. She was so pretty without even trying. "I'll catch you later." He felt a nudge against his leg. "Done playing for the night, Clovis?"

"He could use more play and less bacon," Charlie teased.

"It's carrots and long walks for him from now on."

She lowered to a squat and petted the dog, lifting his chin up and taking a closer look at his face. "His eye looks irritated."

It was hard for Trig to squat and not give away his injury. The last thing he wanted was to draw attention to his leg when he felt so normal. "He was scratching at it earlier. I'll keep an eye on it."

Her look of concern vanished and was replaced with a smile. "Let me know if you need me to take a look tomorrow."

"Will do." Part of him wanted to lean forward and kiss her. Not a heated passionate kiss, although that sounded pleasant enough, but a kiss that said thanks for taking a chance and stopping to pick up a stranger.

He found himself leaning forward and pressing his lips to her cheek. "I'll see you around."

Her hand came to her cheek and that's how he left her. "Let's go, Clovis." He walked inside his room and shut the door.

Fifteen minutes later he was unpacked and on his way to Bowie's. Not knowing how Clovis would be around Bowie's dog Bishop or his daughter Sahara, he decided to leave those introductions until tomorrow.

"No whining tonight," he told the dog before he closed the door. Clovis was supposed to be his support animal but Trig had realized early on that the dog needed him just as much. He seemed to have separation anxiety and would whimper if left alone too long.

Cannon met him in the living room and they both walked to the cabin next door.

Seeing Bowie was like going back to the day he lost his leg, but so much happier. He pulled the big man in for a hug. "Thank you, man. I don't know what I'd have done without you."

In true Bowie form, he said, "Bled out."

They sat on the back porch as a light dusting of snow fell around them and watched the tiny fires that flicked on the frozen lake. "People are really out there fishing?"

"Yep. It's actually great if you don't freeze your nuts off in the process." He told Trig the story of the last time he, Cannon, and Dalton went ice fishing. "It was a mass exodus to warm beds and hot women."

A beautiful blonde walked onto the deck and placed a plate of cookies in front of them. Bowie pulled her into his lap.

"This is my amazing wife, Katie. She owns the bakery in town." He offered Trig a cookie.

Trig couldn't believe his buddy had actually settled down. Bowie said he'd never fall in love again because losing the person he'd loved was too painful. Look at him now. He was a husband and a father. Trig swallowed his envy. He couldn't be upset that the man who'd saved his life had gotten one of his own.

"Cannon says you came up here with Charlie?"

Trig nodded. "Yep, my Mustang is stuck in the snow at the bottom of the pass. I'll call for a tow tomorrow."

"We can ask Bobby Williams to make the arrangements. He owns the gas station and car repair shop in town. He'll know who to call."

Trig looked around and sighed. It felt damn good to be among friends. "I'm so happy to be here."

Katie rose from her husband's lap. "I'm heading to bed. I've got to be up to make the muffins early."

Bowie stood with his wife and kissed her long and hard. "I'll get up with the baby."

She laughed. "If I weren't so tired, I'd consider that foreplay." She looked up at Bowie and winked. "It was nice meeting you, Trig. I'll see you tomorrow."

"I'll be here." He looked toward the bed and breakfast and saw a shadow on the deck and knew immediately it was Charlie. It was too tall to be Sage and didn't have enough limbs to be one of the dogs. "What's Charlie's story?" he asked. Although he thought the question, it somehow made it out of his mouth aloud.

"Hard to say," Cannon started. "She's been gone a long time—like ten years. Her mother died, and she couldn't handle it so she left for college and never came back."

"She got family here?"

Both the brothers said yes at the same time.

Cannon silenced himself with a cookie and Bowie continued. "Not unlike my story, I imagine. Someone she loved died and she couldn't live in the place that reminded her of the loss."

"But now she's back?"

Cannon swallowed. "Her dad is the local doctor. There's more to it, but rumor has it she blamed him for her mother's death. Like somehow he should be capable of saving everyone."

He sipped the beer Bowie had handed him the second he arrived. "It's easy to blame others when life doesn't go your way."

Bowie emptied his bottle and reached into the cooler for three more. "It's easy to lie to yourself when the truth hurts so much." They all popped the caps off the new beers and toasted to friendship and truth.

It was two hours and three additional beers later when Trig stumbled back to his room. He turned the light on and found it empty.

"Clovis? Come here, boy." He searched his space thoroughly and began to worry. Had he somehow gotten loose? A basset hound was no match for the wilds of the Colorado mountains. "Clovis?" he repeated in a whispered yell.

He stopped to listen and heard the soft yelp of his dog. He followed the noise next door to Charlie's room. He didn't understand how his dog had gotten into her space.

He tapped at the door lightly, hoping she was still up, but no light shone from beneath the door. He didn't want to barge in and steal his dog back, but somehow the damn pup had ended up where he shouldn't be. He turned the handle, expecting it to be locked but found it wasn't.

He managed one step inside then tripped over something and found himself on the floor.

A light flickered on and Charlie stood in front of him dressed in nothing but pink panties and a T-shirt. God was she gorgeous. The woman was all legs until his eyes found the rounded curve of her perfect ass. He took her in from her red toenail polish to her pebbled nipples poking against the shirt.

"Wow, you are so damn hot."

He expected her to ignore him. Most women did, but what he saw on Charlie's face confused him until he followed her line of sight.

She was staring at his left leg, which was turned at an odd angle.

"Oh my God, you're hurt. Don't move. It's broken." She fell to her knees and reached for his leg.

The last thing Trig wanted was sympathy. "I'm fine," he grumbled. He reached down and twisted his prosthetic leg so it was back to facing the correct direction.

"You're not fine. You fell, and that's got to hurt."

He was far too drunk to have a filter. "Like a son of a bitch, but that was years ago." He hopped to his feet and limped to the door. "I just want my dog. Save your pity party for someone else."

She fisted her hips, which only drew his attention to her curves. "Your dog cried from the minute you left. The only way to get some sleep was to invite him into my bed."

Trig looked at Clovis and said "Lucky bastard" before he hobbled back to his room with Clovis following closely behind.

CHAPTER FIVE

She knew Trig was hurt. She'd never seen a leg twisted in such a way and not be broken. When he turned it around and it snapped back into place her stomach churned.

Her fingers hovered over the keys of her phone. Did she dare call her father to come and look at Trig? He seemed unhappy with her concern and yet as a doctor, even though she cared for animals, she felt she had a moral obligation to make sure he was all right.

She pressed in her father's number and waited for him to answer.

"Where do I need to be?" he asked.

That was her father's MO. He never asked why, he simply showed up.

"Daddy? It's Charlie, and I need you."

She listened as he gasped. In the background came Agatha's voice. "What's wrong?"

"It's Charlie," he whispered. "She's in trouble."

Charlie could picture her father at this moment brushing his salt and pepper hair away from his eyes and searching for his glasses.

"Daddy, I'm not in trouble, but I need you to come to B's Bed and Breakfast. There's a man here who's taken a fall, and I think he's too drunk to realize he's broken his leg. Can you come?"

There was a moment of silence. "B's? You're at B's?"

She heard a commotion in the background. "Yes, I came to surprise you for Christmas, but if you're—"

"I'm on my way." His keys jingled in the background. "Stay there, sweetheart. Daddy will be there in a few minutes."

Her heart did a flip. How could she have stayed away from him for so long? While she was happy he was on his way, she was angry with herself for wasting so much precious time.

She pulled on a pair of sweatpants and a sweatshirt before she went to the room next door and knocked. "Trig?"

She knocked again and listened. If it weren't

for the low growl of Clovis, she would have thought the room was empty.

"Trig, I've called my father. He's a doctor."

"I don't need a doctor. I hate doctors, hospitals. I hate it all. I'm fine."

She was just about to twist the handle when she heard her father's old diesel truck pull up out front. She raced to the door so no one else was woken up and steered her father to the room at the end of the hallway. He stopped for a second and took her in.

"I can't believe you're back. I'm so...so—"

"I know, Dad, I'm so happy too. I'm sorry it's taken me this long to figure out that I was acting like a child."

She looked up to her father's aged face. What once had been smooth skin was now furrowed with deep lines of worry. His salt and pepper hair had turned marshmallow white. Creped hands pulled her in for a hug. "Let's see to this young man you say is injured, and then we'll get reacquainted." His free hand ran down her arm to grip her hand. "I'm so happy you're home, sweetheart."

"I am home," she said with conviction. Maybe that had been the problem all along. She'd never been able to find herself in a place that felt like home.

Her father tapped on the door but didn't wait for an answer. He twisted the knob and walked inside. Charlie followed. Seconds later, Clovis bounced at the end of the bed. While he looked happy to see her, he barked at her father, which brought Sage and Cannon to the door.

"What's going on?" Sage asked. She went straight into nurse mode and walked inside, taking in the situation. She rushed into the adjoining bathroom to wash her hands.

Charlie leaned against the door and took in Trig, who rose from the mattress like Titan from the sea, all bare and muscular and scarred.

"What the hell?" he yelled.

Charlie walked forward. She had a hard time pulling her eyes from his chest. The man was toned and torn. His body had obviously been through a lot. She remembered his duffel bag and knew he'd fought in a war.

"I asked my father to take a look at you."

She pulled her eyes from the longest scar, which ran from the bottom of his ribs to what her friends would call the happy trail—the thin line of hair leading from his belly button to the treasures hidden beneath the sheet.

"I told you I was fine." He rearranged the bedding. "I don't need a doctor to look at something that's not there."

"Please," she pleaded. "It would make me feel better if you just let him take a peek."

"Dammit, what are you, a sadist? You want to see? Isn't it enough that I had to lose the damn thing and now I have to satisfy your morbid curiosity?" Trig gripped the quilt on the bed and tossed it aside to show that his left leg was missing below the knee.

"Oh, shit," Charlie said. "I had no idea. I'm so sorry."

Trig tilted his head in confusion. "Now you know. As you can see I'm fine. Now you all can leave."

"Now wait a minute, son."

Cannon chuckled. "That's my cue to leave. You're about to get schooled. Let's go, sweetheart." He wrapped his arm around Sage and led her back into the hallway.

Charlie couldn't help the smile that lifted her lips. She'd forgotten the 'now son' talks her father gave the boys. That phrase was only pulled out when he had a lesson to teach.

"I'm not your son," Trig replied.

Her father sat on the edge of the bed. "Nope, because if you were, you'd have better manners." He looked at his daughter. "My daughter was only concerned that you had hurt yourself. Don't go getting your knickers twisted because she called me. That's what daughters are supposed to do. They call their fathers."

Charlie didn't miss the message in that either. It was her father telling her that she should have called sooner. Like ten years sooner.

"While I'm here, I'm going to look at that leg." He stood and leaned over Trig to take in his injury.

Charlie couldn't help but want to look too. "Do you care if I help my father?"

Trig narrowed his eyes. "By all means, take pictures and show the whole town."

Her father manipulated the joint and took a closer look at the scar. "Mighty fine work you got here."

"Compliments of Uncle Sam," Trig replied dryly.

"Where's your leg?"

Trig frowned. "In Afghanistan, I imagine."

Charlie was taken aback when her father cuffed him upside the head. "You know what I meant. Let me see your prosthetic leg."

Trig grumbled as he rubbed his red ear. "It's over there." He pointed to the chair in the corner.

Her father walked to where the leg lay tucked under Trig's folded jeans. "This is what they gave you?"

Trig shook his head. "No, it's the first version. I have two others that fit better. This is loose and so when I'm in the car, it doesn't put a lot of pressure on my scar tissue."

Doc walked back and sat on the other side of Trig—the side closest to his amputated limb. He rubbed at the sore spot where a bruise was blooming.

"This is going to be sore for a few days."

Trig sighed. "I've dealt with worse."

Charlie's father placed his hand on Trig's shoulder and gave it a squeeze. "Thank you for your service. I can't imagine what it feels like to lose something as valuable as a limb, but don't let it take something more valuable away. You are no less of a man than you were the day this happened."

She watched as Trig's eyes grew big. "Thank you, sir." He turned to Charlie. "Not everyone feels like you do."

Charlie's father rose. "No one else matters. View yourself as whole and no one will ever call you a liar." He picked up his bag from the floor and walked to the door. "You coming, Charlie?"

Charlie followed her father. She turned around and looked at Trig, who had pulled Clovis into his arms. "I'll be back to say goodnight."

She closed the door behind her and followed her father to the living room.

"Charlie, it's good to see you, sweetheart." Her father wasted no time in wrapping his arms around her again. This time there wasn't a patient waiting, so he held on to her for a long while.

"I'm so sorry I waited so long."

"But you're here now. That's all that matters."

"You look great, Dad." She pulled him to the couch and sat next to him. "How are you feeling?"

He smiled. "I was feeling old, but now I'm feeling ten years younger. What got you here?"

"Agatha."

Her father's white brows lifted toward the ceiling. "That one is a meddler, but she's a good woman."

"I'm glad you found someone." Charlie could see that he was struggling with what to say about Agatha.

"No one will ever replace your mother." He cupped her face and smiled.

"No, but that doesn't mean there's not room in your big heart for another." Charlie never thought she'd be able to say those words, but seeing her father made her want everything that was good in the world to come his way, including love.

"What about you? Is there anyone special in your life?"

The first person to come to her mind was Trig. It was a silly thought because she didn't know him, but she did think he was special, and it had nothing to do with his missing leg.

"No, I think it's hard to find love in this world."

He laughed boldly and vibrantly. "I'm not too old, and I'm not blind. You've grown up to be a beautiful woman. You look so much like your mother. There's no doubt you're turning heads everywhere you go." He looked over his shoulder toward the hallway. "Hell, you knocked that poor man off his leg."

Charlie smiled. "He seems like a nice guy."

"Couldn't say, I've only seen his surly side, but I imagine he's had a tough go of it." Her father looked into her eyes. "People are quick to judge and slow to forgive."

Charlie knew that was a message to her. "I'm learning."

Doc rose from the couch. "Aren't we all? Let's meet at the diner in the morning for breakfast. Dalton makes the best pancakes in town."

"Dalton Black is still here?"

Her father nodded. "Where else would he go? There's nothing you can't find in Aspen Cove, including good pancakes."

Charlie walked her father to the door. "I love you, Daddy."

"Love you too, Charlie girl."

She lifted to her tiptoes to plant a kiss on lips she hadn't felt in a decade. When she closed the door, she wandered back to Trig's room. She opened the door and was greeted by silence and darkness.

"Good night, Trig," she whispered. Just as she closed the door she added, "I'm not who you think I am. I'm not going to hurt you."

CHAPTER SIX

Sweat rolled off his forehead as Trig sat up with his heart lodged inside his throat. He rarely had dreams or flashbacks, but when they hit him, it was like being dipped into the fiery cauldrons of hell.

He tossed the covers from his body and let the cool morning air wash over his skin. Clovis lifted his head and gave Trig a one-eyed stare. One-eyed because his right eye was swollen shut.

"Hey boy, what did you get into?" When they had left California, Clovis was fine. He'd slept for most of the trip and only gotten out when he needed to pee. Trig considered the diet change, but could he be allergic to carrots? Maybe it was the grain-free salmon kibble. The damn stuff cost thirty bucks a bag, so it better not be the dog food.

He pulled the dog to his chest. At close to seventy-five pounds it wasn't an easy feat.

"Let me see that eye."

Trig gave it a good look and knew he'd have to find a veterinarian. He thought about Charlie, but after the way he'd behaved last night, Charlie was the last person he wanted to see.

Had he heard her correctly when she peeked into his room last night? She had whispered something about not being who he thought she was. Hell, all women were who he thought they were. They were the only subjects he didn't lie to himself about. He'd never be anyone's everything because there were pieces of him physically and emotionally that he'd never get back.

He thought about his girlfriend. The one he had when it all went down. She was a soldier like him. She knew the risks and despite knowing, she'd still walked away.

He'd never forget her last words. "I can't be with you. When they took your leg, they took my dreams."

Like Trig, Lila was a fitness fiend, and she never missed the big marathons. It was why he'd trained so hard for the Rock and Roll Marathon. He knew she'd be there.

He petted Clovis' soft fur as he closed his eyes and remembered the look on her face when he'd raced past her. She'd struggled to keep up but caught up to him after the race.

"Wow, look at you," she'd said. "You're in great shape." That's when he realized that to Lila, he was simply arm-candy. The more people that came over to introduce themselves, the closer she got to him.

"I lost some weight," he'd replied.

"Really? You look just as fit and sexy as always."

"No, really, I took off a hundred and ten pounds of careless bitch." He left her there with her mouth hanging open. It wasn't his finest moment, but it had felt good. One more look at Clovis and he was up and moving.

While he wasn't keen on seeking the help of Charlie, he loved his dog more than he feared her rejection.

Once showered and dressed, he put on his good leg and ventured into the kitchen where coffee was made, and muffins along with fruit, yogurt, and a crockpot of something sat on the table.

"It's breakfast casserole," Cannon said from behind him. "I made it, so it's safe to eat."

"You making the dish is the deciding factor?"

He took a disposable cup from the counter and poured a cup of morning happiness.

"If you tasted anything Sage made, you'd understand. Although, now that the culinary school is open, and they sell take and bake, no one has been poisoned or starved to death."

Trig opened the pot and the smell of bacon, eggs, and cheese greeted him. At his foot, Clovis whined because while he didn't see it, he smelled the bacon, and there was little he wouldn't do for a bite.

"Not for you, buddy. All you get is a bowl of kibble."

Cannon showed him the pantry where they'd put Clovis' food. He poured him a bowl, only to have the dog sniff it and walk away.

"What's with his eye?"

"I'm not sure. I think he might have poked it when he rushed to the woods to pee yesterday. Is there a vet nearby?"

Cannon laughed. "Yep, but she left for the diner about an hour ago. Other than Charlie, there's no one. You'd have to go to Copper Creek or Silver Springs. Both over the pass, and it's still snowing."

Trig looked out the window toward the lake. There was at least six more inches of snow since he'd climbed into bed.

Cannon held his cell phone to his ear. "Hey Charlie, can you take a look at Clovis? His eye looks pretty bad."

Trig did everything he could to stop Cannon from asking.

"Let me talk to her." He really had no choice. Clovis needed care, and Trig was stuck in the mountains without a car.

Cannon handed over the phone.

"Hey Charlie, sorry to bother you. I know you're getting reacquainted with your dad, but do you think you can take a peek at Clovis' eyes at some point?"

"Good morning, Trig, hang on a sec." He heard muffled conversation, but couldn't make out the words. "Bring him to the clinic."

"You sure?"

"You need me to come and get you?"

Trig took another glance out the window. He knew his dog would never make the mile or so walk into town. That's when Cannon shook a set of keys in front of his face. He swiped them and mouthed the words 'Thank you'. "Nope, I've got it. On Main Street, right?"

She gave him the directions and Trig hung up.

"You sure you won't need your truck?"

"Nope, I'll be in the garage whittling last-minute ornaments for Katie's family. They single handedly buy everything I make. Next summer, Sage and I are going to build a dock. Maybe we'll even get a boat someday with the money I earn from those ornaments alone."

"What's that feel like?"

Cannon pulled the top off of a muffin. A chunk dropped to the floor. Clovis wasted no time in gobbling it up. He couldn't be upset at the dog. Food always comforted an injury. Hell, Trig had gone on the no-peanut-butter-cup-left-behind diet for almost three months until he figured out the extra weight would never be a good thing for his current condition. That's when he went on the carrot and salmon plan like Clovis, but Trig's came in filets.

He carried his dog to the truck and got him situated before he climbed inside and gave the key a turn. The truck coughed and sputtered and spit a black cloud of smoke into the frigid air. He backed out and headed for town.

As he pulled into the parking spot in front of the pharmacy, he caught sight of Charlie out of the corner of his eye.

She smiled as she approached and opened his door. "Have you eaten?"

Warm feelings flooded his senses. She'd

never once glanced at his leg when he exited the truck. Her eyes stayed on his face.

"I had some of the breakfast casserole Cannon made."

"Tomorrow you have to have pancakes with me." She pointed at Maisey's Diner. "Dad was right, Dalton makes the best pancakes ever."

"You're asking me to breakfast?"

She reached past him and hefted Clovis from the seat. "Seems neighborly since I did steal your dog and then booby-trap my room so you couldn't take him back."

"Booby-trap?"

She hugged Clovis to her chest. Damn dog was getting the full-on cleavage crush and Trig felt a bit jealous. Maybe he should poke his eye and see if she hugged him to her breasts. He hated thinking about her breasts because that brought thoughts of her jumping out of bed last night in nothing but a thin T-shirt and panties. And he saw those perky nipples jutting out like they were offering themselves up for a taste.

She readjusted Clovis. The dog had to weigh almost as much at her. "I'm careless with my stuff. I dropped my suitcase by the door and fell into the bed."

"You did change."

She blushed. "Generally, I wear more to bed,

but I was too tired to bother. Sorry you got an eyeful."

"Thanks for the eyeful. Best view of the day." He followed her to the pharmacy. Off to the right, there was a waiting room.

"This wasn't here when I left. There used to be a hallway lined with folding chairs, but since Lydia came on board, there have been a lot of changes."

Trig moved through the empty waiting room and into an exam room. It smelled of antiseptic and fear. He hated hospitals and doctors' offices.

"Who's Lydia?"

"Oh, I guess she's Sage's sister and they help run the clinic. They stay open Monday through Thursday. Since it's Friday, we don't have to wait for a room."

Charlie put Clovis on an exam table. "Can you hold him so he doesn't fall off?"

She rummaged through some drawers until she found what she wanted. Trig watched her every move. "I'm sorry I was short with you last night. I'm sensitive about my condition."

She laughed. "I would be too if I were tall and sexy. It's not a condition I suffer from, but I can see what a bummer that would be."

He held the dog while she opened his eyes and took a look. She searched her father's cabinets for some drops. "Made for humans but it should work." She held up the dropper bottle. "It's a dye that will let me see if his cornea is scratched. That's my guess."

"Makes sense. He yelped when he ran into the woods to do his business."

"Pine needle probably." She opened his eye and put a few drops inside. Poor Clovis pawed at her hand until she gave him a firm reprimand and he settled down.

"Can we back up a few seconds?"

She looked up at him and smiled. "You want to backtrack to my lack of clothes or you being hot and sexy?" She pulled some ophthalmic ointment from a cabinet and laid a rope of it under the dog's eyelid.

"Now I'm hot, tall, and sexy." He liked this woman more each minute because, while she knew he was less, she made him feel like he was more.

She stood back and looked at him. "Yes, I'd say all three of those are accurate descriptors." She gave Clovis a pat on the head. "He should be okay, but let's keep an eye on it anyway. Infection is always possible and dangerous."

"Roger that," Trig said. He knew all about infection. There were points in his recovery where he thought he'd lose his whole leg due to infection. "What do I owe you?" He reached for his wallet.

She walked in front of him and gripped his arms. "How about breakfast tomorrow?"

"That's all you want? Breakfast? Surely I owe more than that."

Her smile lit up the room. "Friends help friends."

He lifted a brow. "Are we friends?"

She giggled. "I've spent more time alone with you than I have with anyone in years. I'd say that's the start of a friendship."

"What about guys? Surely you have a boyfriend."

She let out a laugh so loud it startled Clovis. "I'm not really great with men."

"You like women?"

She shook her head. "No, I mean as friends for sure. I love men, but I had so many issues with my dad that I knew I'd never be able to have a relationship until I made amends with him."

"Daddy issues?" He picked Clovis up and hugged him to his chest.

"No, trust issues."

Trig nodded. He knew a great deal about trust issues. "I get it."

She sprayed the table and cleaned up the

mess she'd made. "What about you? You have a girlfriend?"

It was his time to laugh. "I have trust issues, too."

"We're quite the pair, aren't we?" She left the room and they went back into the pharmacy, where an older woman stood behind the register. Charlie reached for two packages of peanut butter cups. "What's your poison?" she asked.

"Brunettes who love dogs, peanut butter and chocolate," he mumbled. He reached for his wallet and paid for Charlie's candy.

"You must be Trig," the older woman said. She turned to Charlie. "You're right. He is handsome."

"Thanks, Agatha. Nothing like embarrassing a girl." She palmed the candy bars and rushed outside.

Trig followed close behind. "You're embarrassed?"

"Well, I should be, but I can't be upset at her. She's the one that got me to come back to Aspen Cove."

"Maybe I should go in and give her a big thank you hug and kiss."

Charlie walked to Cannon's truck. She pulled her lower lip into her mouth. "You could or you could kiss me."

Trig nearly dropped Clovis. He barely got him into the car before he turned around. "You want me to kiss you?"

She stared at his lips. "Crazy, right? But I kind of do."

"Kind of?"

She rolled her pretty blue eyes. "Do you want me to beg?"

"That might be nice." When was the last time a woman begged him for anything?

"You may be all those things I said earlier, but you're not nice."

He pulled her to his chest. "I can be real nice if properly motivated." He lifted her chin and brushed his lips across hers. She tasted like honey and happiness. For the first time in a long time Trig felt the warmth of hope ease into his heart.

CHAPTER SEVEN

What the hell was she doing? "Oh my God. I'm so sorry. Maybe it's the altitude. The lack of oxygen. I don't ask strangers to kiss me."

Trig wrapped his arms around Charlie's waist. "We're not strangers."

"I know, but I don't know you well, and I don't want you to think I'm cheap or easy."

Trig chuckled. "Cute, sexy, and forgiving are the words I thought of first. Cheap or easy never crossed my mind." He thumbed her chin so she was forced to look at him. "While I'd love to kiss you—really kiss you, I'll wait until you ask me again. I'm a good kisser, Charlie. You won't want to miss one." He smiled and opened the truck door, then climbed inside, leaving the door ajar.

She let out a disappointed breath. "My last kiss was awful."

"Who did you kiss?"

Her head hung. "It's not that I kissed him. More like he trapped me under the mistletoe and kissed me."

"I can't blame the guy. Who wouldn't want to kiss you? Tell you what, rather than ask, I'll wait for you to kiss me." He touched his soft full lips. "These will be waiting and ready when you are."

"But I don't ask strangers to kiss me."

Trig looked behind her toward the bakery. "Let's get a muffin and better acquainted." He turned toward his dog. "You'll be okay, buddy."

She watched as he cracked the window open, climbed out of the truck, and closed the door behind him. "It's Friday, and I'm told that means it's raspberry muffin day." He threaded his hand through her arm and walked her to B's Bakery. He stopped outside and gently brushed off the few flakes of snow that had fallen on her hair. They entered to find Katie behind the counter.

"Couldn't get enough of them, could you?" She plated up a few muffins, cookies, and one big dark chocolate brownie. "Two coffees?"

They both nodded, and Katie made two cups

and brought them to the table under a corkboard labeled 'The Wishing Wall'. "I'll be in the back mixing if you need me." She disappeared and left them alone.

"Brownies are my favorite." Charlie picked off the crunchy edge and devoured it in seconds.

"You like brownies. What else?" Trig picked up a Christmas tree-shaped sugar cookie.

Seeing shaped Christmas cookies made her think of her mother. "I used to make cookies every year with my mother. On Christmas Eve, we'd sit outside and make a wish on the North Star."

"I like cookies, so we have that in common." He broke the Christmas tree in half and offered it to her.

"I miss my mother."

"I don't miss mine. I love her, but since my accident, she treats me like I'm handicapped."

Charlie cocked her head to the right. "But..." She didn't want to point out that he was missing part of his leg. Her mother had hovered over her when she got a splinter, so she couldn't imagine how Phyllis Parker would have behaved if something serious had happened.

"Don't say it. I hate being viewed as different from other people."

Charlie swiped the rest of the cookie from

his hand. "You are different." She waited to see the frown she knew he'd give her. "You're tall, hot and sexy and you know what? I didn't even know you were missing part of your leg until you threw a temper tantrum last night and tossed off the blankets. I enjoyed the show, by the way."

He moved closer. "There you go again with the hot and sexy."

She leaned in and said, "Don't forget tall."

He reached up and touched her hair. "Does my missing leg bother you?"

"A lot less than it bothers you."

He looked above her head. She turned to watch him reach for the sticky notes and pen. "You're supposed to write down a wish. I figure since it's almost Christmas, this should be perfect."

He scribbled on the note, folded it in half, and pinned it to the wall.

She sat and stared at the piece of paper. There were so many things to wish for, but she didn't need a note to get her wish. She looked around the bakery and hoped no one walked inside. She moved her chair so she sat next to Trig with their thighs touching.

"I don't need to wish for what I want. All I need to do is ask." She turned to face him. "Trig Whatley, show me what a good kisser you are."

"You ready for the best kiss of your life?"

She gave him a subtle nod and then lifted her chin and closed her eyes. She smiled and leaned toward him until his lips touched hers in a feather-light kiss. The soft and supple caress combined with the feel of him being so near created an intoxicating effect. She inched closer and he brought his hand up to cup the back of her head. Her heart beat so hard she was certain he could hear it. Her fingers pressed against his firm chest and she felt his heart keeping beat with hers.

He pulled away only long enough to look at her lips and kiss her again. Kissing Trig was like nothing she'd ever experienced. It was lust and hunger wrapped up together to create an intense heat.

Charlie hadn't known what to expect given her last kiss was so bad, but she didn't expect to want to reciprocate so enthusiastically. Their tongues touched and tasted and tantalized one another. Without thought, her fingers threaded through his hair.

Lost in each other, they didn't hear Katie until she let out a giggle. "Need a room? I've got an empty apartment upstairs."

Charlie wanted to climb under the table. She

buried her face in her hands. "Oh lord, how embarrassing."

Trig sat back and smiled. "That wasn't embarrassing. That was amazing."

"But..." Charlie looked at Katie, who had picked up their near empty plate and walked away.

Trig moved so close their foreheads touched. "I know her husband, and I know they kiss."

"On the first date?" She lowered her head until it fell against his chest. When she inhaled, she breathed him in. He smelled like fresh snow, cedar, and something uniquely male.

"Is this a date?" Trig asked.

Charlie groaned and pulled away. "Oh hell, I'm sorry. I don't know what this is. Maybe it's simply me trying to forget my boss kissing me under the mistletoe at our Christmas party."

"Your boss? That must have been awkward."

"It was awful, and then the last few days, he's been chasing me around the clinic."

Trig stretched out his injured leg and rubbed where his prosthetic was attached. "I'm a good shot. You want me to take him out or just graze him?"

"I took care of it." Instinctually, she reached down and massaged his leg. "I quit."

He lowered his hands to hers. She was certain he'd make her stop, but he didn't; he simply moved her fingers to where his joint hurt.

"Massage is great therapy. I do a lot of muscle work on animals with torn ACLs and amputations." She winked at him. "You're just a bigger animal."

"I generally don't like people touching my leg."

"But you'll let me?"

He leaned back and picked up his coffee. "We did kiss, so if I trusted you with my lips then I suppose I could trust you with my leg or what's left of it."

"Do most people treat you differently because of it?"

"You'd be surprised. At first I felt like a circus act. I got used to the stares, but it's the intimacy that's the worst. You get to know a girl and then you get to that point where it's the next step and they can't handle it."

Charlie thought about it for a minute. "I want to ask you something, but I don't want you to get mad at me."

He gave her a cautious look but nodded. "Go ahead, but no guarantees."

Charlie didn't want to ruin what they'd started. While she knew there was little hope of it going anywhere, she'd done a great deal of soul searching since Agatha Guild had reached out to her. She realized that she often sabotaged herself and wondered if Trig did the same.

"So...do you think it's their apprehension or because they feed into yours? My father was right last night when he told you to view yourself as whole and no one would ever call you a liar."

He smiled. "I hear you have your own issues. Do you want to talk about why you didn't come home for ten years?"

"I suppose it's no secret." She knew he was deflecting, but she also got the feeling that Trig was the kind of man who would think about what she asked before he had an answer.

"Seems like you came to terms with it."

She looked at her hands resting on his thigh. "Sure. It was like you losing your leg: you accept the loss, but you never truly recover. I was young and stupid. I pretty much lost both of my parents at once. It was unfathomable to believe my father couldn't save her. I felt so much remorse and guilt for blaming him that I stayed away. On some level, I blamed myself. She got so mad at me that day. Maybe I got her blood pressure up."

"You can't blame yourself. Life happens and death is part of the journey." He cupped her cheek and pressed his lips to hers. It wasn't a passionate kiss, but one that said he understood.

"You never really know what you have until it's gone. One thing I learned from this accident is to appreciate the minutes more."

"What will you do with the ones you've got? Do you have plans?" She lifted her hand, but he pressed it back to his leg.

"I left California to find myself." He pinched her chin gently. "Looks like I found you instead."

"Ha. If I remember correctly, I found you and your dog on the side of the road."

They both looked toward Cannon's truck. Clovis was standing on his back legs looking straight toward them. "Speaking of my dog. He suffers from separation anxiety. I should get back to him."

Charlie laughed. "Are you sure you're not his support human?"

Trig pulled Charlie in for a hug. "I'm not sure of anything anymore."

CHAPTER EIGHT

Charlie stood on the sidewalk and watched Trig take off toward the bed and breakfast. She touched her kiss-swollen lips and smiled. Trig Whatley didn't lie. He was a damn good kisser.

Agatha stuck her head out the door and said, "I'm making cookies. Do you want to help?"

Charlie's heart did a flip. Lots of people make Christmas cookies but that was something she had done with her mother.

"No, but I'll come up and watch."

Agatha nodded and led her to the small apartment above the pharmacy.

"How long has my father lived here?" So much had changed.

The older woman moved around the kitchen

gathering supplies. Flour, sugar, butter, salt and every color of sprinkle known to man sat on the Formica counter. "He's been here ever since I've known him." Agatha poured ingredients into the bowl by sight. That was how Charlie's mother had cooked. It was always a pinch of this and a plop of that but somehow the cookies were always perfect. Just went to show that the recipe for success wasn't rigid. A person could stray from the intended path and still wind up with something good.

When the initial sugar cookie dough was finished Charlie stuck her finger into the bowl to grab a taste. It melted on her tongue and left a bittersweet memory.

"Do you know what happened to our house on Jasmine Lane?"

"It's still there. Your father rented it to Marina for a while but she married the sheriff, so they live next door with their little one, Kellyn."

"So the house is vacant now?"

Agatha wrapped plastic wrap over the bowl and put it in the refrigerator to cool. She brought back a bowl of already chilled dough. "Yes, for now, but with so many people coming back to town, he won't have a problem renting it."

"Oh. There did seem to be a lot of growth. I saw the Dry Goods Store is open all year round as well as the diner. Kathy's Cut and Curl is now Cove Cuts. There's been a lot of change."

Agatha spread plastic wrap on the table and handed Charlie a cold marble rolling pin. She took it without thought and began to flatten the cookie dough on the surface. They worked together much the same way Charlie and her mother had all those years ago.

"Change is the only certainty in life. That and the fact that your butt will get bigger if you eat too many cookies."

"How did you meet my father?"

Charlie knew the Guilds had a long-term presence in the town but she wanted specifics.

Agatha sat next to her with an array of cookie cutters shaped in trees, wreaths and snowmen. "I knew him when I was a child but I left town to go to school. I traveled a great deal and when I moved back, I lived in Silver Springs. Your dad would show up to square dancing every so often and I'd always make sure I was his partner, and then one day fate stepped in. Dalton crashed his motorcycle and I brought him back to town so he could see your father for his injuries. That was the beginning of the beginning. Then there was the fire and I took care of your pops while he recovered."

Charlie was grateful for the woman's love

and care. Had it not been for her, she might not have known her father had been injured. "Was he a gracious patient?"

Agatha laughed. "He was as friendly as a cat on fire."

"Sounds like you deserve a medal."

"Men are an interesting species. They want to be babied, but at the same time, they don't want you to forget they're men."

After listening to Trig talk about feeling less than a man with his injury, Charlie knew Agatha knew the secret sauce to a man's heart.

"Do you love my father?"

The older woman blushed. "Oh, yes. There's no doubt. Does that bother you?"

While she thought it would, it didn't. How could she expect her father to stay single and lonely his whole life? Hell, she was only twenty-eight and she was lonely.

"No, I'm glad he found you."

Agatha smiled. "I'd like to believe I found him. What about you? Do you have a boyfriend?"

Charlie's hand went straight to her lips. She closed her eyes and relived the one perfect kiss of her life.

"No, there's no one special." The words felt like a bitter lie in her mouth. She didn't want to start a relationship with Agatha on an untruth. "I did kiss Trig Whatley today." She sighed in that dreamy way girls do when their hearts are full. "It was a perfect kiss."

Agatha got up to put the first tray of cookies in the oven. On her way back, she grabbed the percolator and two cups. "This story needs coffee and sweets. Tell me more. What made it so good?"

There wasn't one thing she could pinpoint, but it had been amazing. "I suppose it was because kissing him was my choice." She hadn't considered it before, but Trig didn't force himself on her like Evan. He merely promised her the best kiss of her life and delivered on that promise.

"It should always be your choice." Agatha narrowed her eyes. "Has anyone forced themselves on you? I've got a gun, and I'm a very good shot, you know."

Charlie laughed. "Now you sound like Trig, and yes, my boss caught me under the mistletoe. It wasn't pleasant."

By the way Agatha pressed the cutters into the dough, it was obvious she wasn't happy to hear that news either. "You need a new boss."

"Yes, I do. I quit my job just before I left town."

A smile bloomed a mile wide. "That's wonderful news. You can stay here and practice. Your father is tired of tending to animals."

"He takes care of animals, too?"

"Not willingly, but when Lloyd Dawson had a breach birth with his prize heifer, he called your dad. Sage had a bird with a broken wing and your father patched that up. Given that the town is full of special needs pets, you'd stay busy here."

Charlie considered her statement, but knew it would never work. She didn't want her father to think she came back to town because she had no other options. She came back because it was time to make everything right again.

"Otis isn't the only special needs animal?"

The timer went off and Charlie jumped up to take the perfectly baked cookies from the oven.

"Oh gosh no. Cannon has a one-eyed cat, and I swear Bowie's and Katie's dog Bishop has ADD or maybe it's because he's still a puppy. My nephew and his wife Lydia have a retired police dog who has PTSD and some work-related injuries."

"And Clovis has a scratched cornea."

"Trig's fat, squatty dog you worked on at the clinic today?"

"Yep, that's the one."

There was a commotion on the stairs and a moment later Charlie's father walked in. He took in the scene around him and smiled. Charlie wondered what he was thinking.

"What a beautiful sight to see. My two girls chatting it up and making cookies." He walked forward and took a wreath from the tray. Before he took a bite, he kissed Agatha on the lips and Charlie on the cheek. Somehow it all felt right.

"Where have you been?" Charlie asked her father.

He glanced at the living room behind them. Sitting on the floor was a Christmas tree. "I haven't had one in ten years. I thought maybe..." —his expression softened—"maybe you can help me decorate it."

Charlie hated to admit it, but she hadn't had a Christmas tree either. Her heart ached at the thought of celebrating without her mother, but Agatha was right, change was inevitable and even though she hadn't had a tree in a decade that was a change from the way she was brought up. She and her father used to trek into the woods and pick their tree while her mom stayed home and made spiced cider and hot cocoa.

"Did you go to our favorite place and find this one?" Charlie rose from the chair and walked into the living room, where the tree lay on the carpet.

"Oh, no. I'm too old for a trek into the woods but not too old for a trek to Copper Creek." He leaned over and lifted the tree to its stand. "This one is compliments of Angels Tree Farm."

A feeling of giddiness washed over Charlie. How had so much changed, and yet so much seemed familiar? "It's perfect."

Agatha busied herself rearranging the furniture to make room for the tree. Charlie's dad set it in the corner and they all stepped back to admire its perfection and breathe in the scent of pine, sap, and love.

"Charlie, I've still got all the ornaments you made as a kid, but I don't want to stir up memories if you're not ready for them."

She swallowed a lump in her throat. *Was she ready? Would she ever be ready?* She erased the doubt. Memories were simply a time to reflect on the past. If anything, they would remind her of the childhood she'd had. "Let's decorate this tree."

Agatha bounced like a kid. "I'm so excited," she said. "I'll get the cocoa started while you two find the tree jewelry."

Her father stood in front of her and smiled. "I'm so happy you're back." He looked over his shoulder to Agatha, who was already at the stove pouring milk and cocoa into a pan. "She's a good woman, but there's room in my life for both of you."

Charlie was certain her father worried that he'd given her the impression she'd been replaced. "Daddy, I like her. She's so much like Mom and yet different. You did well." She knew it was silly for her to call her father Daddy, but old habits were hard to break.

The rest of the afternoon was spent reliving the memories of each ornament. Agatha added her own flair to the tree by draping it with paper chains and strings of popcorn.

They filled up on cookies and cocoa and watched *A Charlie Brown Christmas*, which was part of Agatha's Christmas traditions. By the end of the evening, Charlie was part of a family again. Though she did feel a twinge of guilt for moving on, she realized that it had been a decade-long process.

"How about breakfast in the morning?" her father asked as he walked her to the door.

Charlie shook her head. "I can't. I've got a date with Trig."

Her father frowned.

"You don't like him?"

Doc Parker shook his head. "I don't know

him well enough to not like him, but I don't like that I've just gotten my daughter back and I might have to share her with another man."

Agatha reached over and pulled her father's ear. "Now Paul, don't be a hypocrite. Charlie just got you back and she's sharing you with me."

It was funny to see her father blush. "You're right, lovey. I've got to learn to share."

Charlie looked at the couple in front of her and said, "Old dog—new tricks."

Agatha laughed. "Sweetheart, they are never too old to train."

CHAPTER NINE

Trig sat on the deck sharing a beer with Cannon. It had been a long time since he'd been this relaxed. He knew his decision to leave California was a wise one. Not in the two years that he'd lived there had he had a kiss like the one he shared with Charlie.

"What's your long-term plan?" Cannon asked.

"I don't have one." He knew his short-term plan was to get his lips on Charlie again as soon as possible, but after that, he had no idea what the future had in store.

"What's your skillset? You got anything to sell to the world?"

Trig chuckled. "Like your brother, I don't

have money problems. I've got a decent pension. What I have is a direction problem. All I know is I want something real."

Cannon emptied his beer and tossed the bottle to the open trash can in the corner. "It doesn't get much more real than Aspen Cove. Bowie has been thinking about expanding the bait and tackle shop to a full outdoor recreation store. If that's your thing, I'm sure he'd love to partner with someone."

Trig rubbed the sore spot on his leg where he'd scraped it in his fall. The small abrasion was hot and angry.

"I don't think I'm cut out for being a cashier. I love the thrill of an adventure."

"No man, that's what he's planning. He wants to hire someone to cashier while he and probably you take clients ice fishing or day treks snowshoeing. Who would be a better role model than a guy who refuses to give in?" Cannon looked at Trig's left leg.

"Seriously? I'd love that." He hadn't given owning a part of something much thought. He'd spent the bulk of his recovery training for the marathon. He'd made his point to Lila, and now he had to make a point to himself.

He considered Charlie's statement about whether he thought people came to their own conclusions about him, or if he was feeding their fears and making his predictions come true. One thing he knew was if he didn't believe in himself, he couldn't expect anyone else to.

"I'm sure he'll broach the subject while you're here, so don't tell him I prepped you."

"No worries. I can keep things to myself."

The door opened and out walked Charlie. "You boys want privacy?"

Trig nearly fell out of his chair to make room for her. "No, come and have a seat. I warmed it up for you."

Cannon looked between the two of them and smiled. "I was going inside anyway. See you in the morning." He walked inside, leaving them alone.

Charlie searched the snow-covered deck. "Where's Clovis?"

Trig nodded toward the window where they could see Otis in his dog bed curled around the oversized hound. "He's traded me in. He saw me kissing you and has given me the cold shoulder ever since."

"How's his eye?"

"Still swollen shut, but he managed to find both his and Otis' bowl of kibble so I think he'll survive."

"I love a survivor."

86

Trig looked at his half-full beer and offered it to Charlie. "You want a drink?"

"Thanks." She took it and water-falled it into her mouth.

"Afraid of catching something? Need I remind you that we shared a kiss earlier?"

She pressed her lips to the top of the bottle and took a deep drink. "That wasn't just a kiss. That was a landmark event." She looked down at the bottle. "I was being considerate. For all you know, I'll backwash."

He chuckled. "For all you know, I already did."

She wrapped her arms around her body and shivered. "I forgot how cold it gets up in the mountains." She leaned back and stared toward the sky. "But look at the stars. You won't get this view in the city."

Trig continued to stare at the woman in front of him. "Nope, I've never seen anyone more beautiful."

She lowered her eyes to him and even in the dark of the star-lit night he could see her cheeks pink from his compliment.

"Are you angling for more kisses?"

He walked over and lifted her from the chair, only to change places and put her in his lap. "Are you offering?"

She turned sideways and flung her legs over the arm of the Adirondack chair. "I could be persuaded to kiss you."

He placed one hand on her thigh and the other on her back. "Persuaded, huh? What do I have to do?"

She leaned forward and whispered against his lips. "All you need to do is ask."

"Charlie Parker, will you give me your best kiss?"

She didn't need any more prodding. Sitting on Trig's lap with his hands on her body and her lips on his was the best way to spend a cold December evening. When their mouths met in the middle, she no longer felt cold. He managed to ignite a fire in her veins that blazed through her body.

It wasn't until she squirmed and he winced that they pulled apart. "Are you hurt? Shit, I'm too heavy for you." She tried to hop off his lap, but he held her in place.

"You are not too heavy for me. I'm fine." He pointed to his left leg. "I cut myself when I fell last night. It's a bit sore but it's nothing."

Her lips spread into a thin line. "Are you sure I'm not too heavy?"

"Charlie, you're perfect. I love the way your ass feels in my lap." He shifted so she could feel just how much he liked it. "If I liked the feel of you any better, I'd embarrass myself." The fact that his hard-as-a-rock rod sat stiff between his legs was proof enough that Charlie Parker did something for him.

She rocked against him. "Nothing to be embarrassed about there," she said.

"Glad you think so."

She laid her head on his chest while they both watched the tiny fires of the diehard outdoorsmen on the lake go out. Pretty soon the only lights they saw came from the millions of stars above them. Off in the distance, a shooting star raced across the sky to disappear behind the peak.

"Make a wish," she said.

He turned her head and pressed his forehead to hers. "I already did at the bakery and it came true. I got to kiss you."

Her mouth dropped open. "That was your wish?"

He reached into his pocket and pulled it out. "I took it back since it was already granted."

She snuggled into him. "That was my wish too."

He looked to where the falling star had disappeared and made another wish. Only this one required a whole other level of commitment from Charlie Parker.

"We should get to bed if we plan to have breakfast before I leave tomorrow."

She stiffened in his arms. "You're leaving?"

Was that sadness he heard in her voice?

"Yes." He tapped her nose and rose from the chair setting her on her feet. "But only for the night." He pointed to the ice on the lake. "It's boys' night out, and we're going ice fishing. I'll be back on Christmas Eve."

There was a sigh of relief that made Trig feel good. She'd feel something if he were gone.

"What about Clovis?"

"I was going to take him." He looked back at the house to where the dogs continued to sleep.

"Leave him here. It's bad enough you might freeze to death, but no need to make the dog suffer. You realize there's a big storm coming in."

"Really? How bad?"

"They say it's going to lay down a lot of ice."

"We can handle it."

"Why you'd want to is beyond me, but I'm sure it's testosterone driven." She shrugged. "I'll keep Clovis warm while you guys bond in the freezing cold."

"You'd do that for me?" It warmed his heart that she'd offer.

She pressed her lips against his for a quick kiss. "That's what friends do for friends."

"So now we're friends?"

She turned and walked toward the door. "We have to be. I don't kiss strangers."

He opened the door and limped inside. His leg was really bothering him tonight. "What if I want to be more than friends?"

She looked at him like he was one of her cosmic brownies. The ones she devoured in seconds.

"We can negotiate over pancakes and coffee."

He walked her to her room and gave her another kiss. This one promised the possibility of more.

He went back to the living room to get Clovis, but he didn't have the heart to separate him from Otis. The two dogs had formed a bond.

Trig went to his room and removed his leg. What had been a small scrape earlier had grown into a painful red-hot knot. Trig pulled out the salve he used for sore spots and rubbed the ointment into his skin. He didn't have time for something as silly as this to slow him down. He had ice fishing and kisses to look forward to.

CHAPTER TEN

It wasn't often that Charlie rose from bed the first time her alarm went off. She had a three snooze limit built into her daily schedule, but delaying twenty-one minutes meant she'd have to wait that much longer to see Trig. And twenty-one minutes might as well have been a lifetime.

She tossed off the quilt and hung her legs over the edge of the bed. Had it only been two days since she'd met him? Why was it that some people felt like a comfortable sweater right away and others were like wet, itchy wool?

She pushed off the mattress and landed on the hardwood floor. She padded to the bathroom where she turned on the shower. On the other side of the wall she could hear Trig sing. It was a nice melodic sound that filled the air. He had no idea she could hear him, and she might never tell. Then again…

She lathered herself up as she listened to his rendition of "White Christmas." He changed the words to 'I'm dreaming of a white Christmas where I get my wishes of more Charlie kisses'. How could she not fall a little in love with him?

She'd rushed through her morning routine only to find herself stumped at what to wear. She hadn't come to Aspen Cove looking for anything but redemption. Redemption didn't require nice clothes. She rummaged through her suitcase and picked the most attractive of her unattractive choices. She was stuck with cable knit sweaters and worn jeans, but at least she'd be comfortable.

A look in the mirror showed dark circles under her eyes which she could only blame Trig for since she'd stayed up way too late thinking about his kisses and what he meant when he asked about being more than friends.

She raced from her room to the kitchen were she heard voices and found Cannon and Trig leaning over a list.

"I'll stop by and get the gear from Bowie if you can rummage up some dogs and buns," Trig said. He looked up at Charlie. While he didn't say anything, the light in his eyes and his smile said it all. He was happy to see her. "You ready to get those pancakes?" He walked forward, but she didn't miss the hitch in his step.

"You okay?"

He narrowed his eyes. "Don't baby me, Charlie. I'll let you know if I'm not all right."

She shrugged and left him standing there. "I'll drive since you don't have a car." When she opened the door, she saw his Mustang sitting in the driveway.

He brushed past her. "I'll drive because I do have a car, and the roads are clear for now."

"You're a stubborn man." She walked to the passenger side and reached for the handle.

"Wait up. I open the door for my dates." He rushed to her side.

"It's a good thing," she replied, "because I don't kiss or date men with bad manners."

He opened the door and helped her inside, then he bent over and covered her mouth with his. It was a deep sensual kiss that made her want to exit the car and drag him into her room.

"God, I love your lips." He pulled back and licked the moisture from his.

She couldn't help herself when she broke out into song and repeated his lyrics only this time she added his name. "I'm dreaming of a white

Christmas where I get my wishes for more Trig kisses."

He laughed. "I hate thin walls." He turned the key, and the growl of eight cylinders roared to life. She had to admit there was something sexy about men and muscle cars. Less than five minutes later, they were walking into Maisey's diner. It had been years since she'd seen the woman.

"Charlie Parker, is that you?" Maisey rushed to fold her into a hug. "I'd recognize you any-where." She pinched Charlie's cheek and squealed. "Who's your man?"

Charlie looked at Trig. How was she sup-posed to introduce him? "Hey, Maisey. Oh he's—"

"Trig Whatley ma'am," he said while he gave her a gentle handshake. "Charlie trades kisses for pancakes. I'm here to pay up."

She didn't know if she wanted to laugh or punch him. So she did both. "A girl's got to eat."

Maisey pointed to a back booth and walked away to put in their pancake order.

"You owe me a lot of pancakes, mister." She sat on one side of the booth expecting him to take the other but he slid in next to her. The heat of their touching thighs stirred a hunger that pan-cakes would never quench.

His hand came to rest on her thigh under the table. "You owe me more kisses. I want hundreds of them."

She decided to mess with him. "I don't like pancakes quite that much."

He reached for the napkin holder, which forced him into her space. He turned to her with the whisper of his heated breath next to her ear. "But you like my kisses."

She pressed her lips to his. "Better than pancakes."

He sat back and placed a napkin in front of each of them. "How were you going to explain me to Maisey?"

He sat back and lifted a brow.

"I haven't quite figured out what you and I are yet, so I had no idea."

Maisey arrived with two cups swinging from one hand a pot of coffee from the other. "Pancakes are almost up." The bell above the door rang and in walked a young brunette.

Charlie couldn't believe her eyes.

"Oh my God, that's—"

Maisey turned her head and smiled. "My future daughter-in-law."

"Dalton is engaged to Indigo?"

Maisey waved the woman over. "Samantha" —she pointed to Charlie and Trig—"this is Doc

Parker's daughter, Charlie, and her pancake pimping partner."

A look of knowing came over the pop star's face. "Hey, Charlie, your father is the best. I'm so sorry he was injured fighting my cabin fire." She turned to Trig. "Pancake pimp?"

Trig blushed a little. "What can I say? Charlie drives a hard bargain."

Charlie ignored Trig's jest. All the pieces finally came together. Agatha had only said that her father had been hurt in a fire that burned down Dalton's girlfriend's cabin. Leave it to a senior citizen to leave out the good stuff like Samantha was Indigo and Dalton was her man.

"You built the Guild Center and the new fire department, didn't you?" The longer she stayed in Aspen Cove the more smoothly the pieces fit together.

"I just put up the money, which was the least I could do after the people here made me one of their own."

"Aspen Cove is like that. They take care of each other. And...everyone belongs."

Samantha nodded. "It's great meeting you both." And she was gone.

Charlie turned to Trig and whispered excitedly. "Oh my God, that was Indigo."

He shrugged. "I got nothing."

She elbowed him. "She's like the biggest thing since...I don't know since..."

"Sliced bread?" Trig asked.

Maisey poured them each a cup of coffee and pulled creamers from her pocket. "Here she's just Samantha." The bell above the door rang again, and a waft of chilly air followed a small crowd into the restaurant. They stomped the snow off their boots and greeted Maisey by name. She pointed them to a table on the other side of the restaurant and hurried off to get their menus.

Charlie sipped her coffee. "So much has changed, and so much is the same."

Trig's hand gave her thigh a soft squeeze. "I think it's great that the town is getting a rebirth. Everything changes."

"I suppose you're right."

"Any plans for the rest of the day?"

She hadn't considered anything past pancakes and kisses. "I think I'm going to drive by my old house and then go visit my mom at the cemetery before it gets too cold. You?"

"I need to pick up the fishing supplies after I drop you off. Then I'm going to trek across the ice, drill a hole in it, drop a hook, and try to catch a fish all the while trying to not freeze my nut sack off. I'll have an awful undercooked hotdog while I listen to the guys boast about the last fish they didn't catch. All the while, I'll think about you. I'll probably stare at the sky and wish we were back on the deck. I'll regret saying yes to ice fishing when I'd rather be warm in bed with you."

A quiver ran through her body and it had nothing to do with his talk about ice. "That's bold talk. Who says I'd invite you to my bed?"

His hand moved way up her thigh until it sat nearly at her heat. "Your body says what your lips refuse to utter."

She prayed the longing she felt in her body didn't show on her face. "That I'd rather be in your bed so I wasn't stuck lying in the wet spot?"

She loved the way his jaw fell slack and his eyes grew wide. "It's a date. Christmas Eve. My bed."

"Deal." She was shocked at how easy everything was with Trig. She imagined a man who nearly lost his life didn't have much time or need for pretenses. And maybe after wasting the last ten years of her life, she was determined to do things differently. "What should I bring for this sleepover?"

Trig's lips lifted into a sly grin. "Oh, sweetheart, don't show up intent on getting sleep. That's not part of the plan."

The warmth of his words washed over her and settled between her thighs. She was certain he could feel the molten heat burning between her legs.

"You're making me—"

"Hot?"

"Here you go, kids. And yes, they're hot." Maisey winked at Charlie. "Although I imagine that's not what you were talking about by the blush on your cheeks." She walked away mumbling something about youth being wasted on the young.

Trig took a bite of his pancakes and moaned. He forked a bite and offered it to Charlie.

"I've got my own," she said.

He touched the syrupy bite to her lips. "Let me feed your hunger. Let me satisfy your needs."

She melted into the booth. "I'm counting on you to do both. Up for the task?"

He took her hand and laid it on his lap. Beneath her fingers she felt just how up he was.

They finished their breakfasts. Charlie got out of the car at the bed and breakfast with a promise to watch Clovis. Trig pulled away, and all she could think about was how long the next twenty-fours hours would be.

Charlie climbed into her Jeep and drove straight for the cemetery. She walked through the snow to her mother's granite tombstone and kneeled before the carved heart. There were five words she had to say. She traced over her mother's name and said, "I love you." She kissed her fingers and touched the cold headstone. "I'm sorry."

There were no more tears to spill. She'd cried a river over the loss of her mother. Tears her mother would have hated because all Phyllis Parker wanted was for her daughter to live, love, and laugh.

While she stood there, the clouds parted and the sun warmed her cheeks for a mere minute, and somehow, it felt like it was a message from her mother to her that all that was broken would mend.

Charlie left the cemetery feeling free. If her mother had been alive, she would have told her to live each day to the fullest. A full life didn't mean to stay in a job with a pervy boss or beat herself up for past mistakes. Charlie had a future and, while she didn't know what that future would look like, she had a feeling that for now, it would include Trig.

CHAPTER ELEVEN

"How far out are we heading?" Trig adjusted his backpack and followed Bowie across the frozen lake. The sun had peeked through the clouds briefly before the storm ate up any warmth it could provide. He was already cold and halfway miserable.

He hadn't carried a rucksack in two years, but the weight felt good on his back. His leg, on the other hand, screamed with every step he took.

"Just to the cove." Bowie pointed to the frozen waterfall. "It's quiet there and the fishing is pretty decent."

Trig pushed through the pain of his prosthesis rubbing against the abraded skin. It served him right for walking into Charlie's room in the dark. He also knew better than to wear his old equipment, but bad habits died hard.

He thought about Charlie on the way to the cove. He'd kissed plenty of women in his day. Less so in the last two years and maybe that's what made her kiss so much more. He could still feel her lips against his. Still taste the honeyed sweetness of her mouth. He loved the way her hands went straight to his chest and then to his hair.

He glanced over his shoulder to where the lights along the shore flickered in the distance. Sage had strung a row of Christmas lights across the deck railing. It helped to distinguish the bed and breakfast from the rest of the houses. Bowie's place was lit up like he was trying to single-handedly finance the electric company.

"I bet they can see your house from space," Trig said.

"It's Sahara's first Christmas. I wanted it to be special."

Cannon stopped in the alcove and spread a tarp on the ice in front of them before he started to unfold the four-man tent. "She's still a baby. Do you think she notices?"

Bowie frowned. "Of course. You should see her eyes light up when we take her outside."

While they set up camp, Trig made quick work of drilling through the ice and sawing a hole the size of a frying pan. If they were lucky that's exactly what they'd be doing for dinner—cooking lake trout on an open fire was the plan.

For the next hour, they dropped their lines into the freezing depths and waited. The wind whipped around them and the sleet fell like razors from the sky.

Trig couldn't get comfortable. He knew things were going downhill fast when he started sweating and got chills, but he ignored the signs. This was his first real guys' night out since the accident. There was no way he was going back to shore.

"So..." Bowie said. "When did you get your medical license?" He stared straight at Trig.

Trig knew he'd only had a single beer so there no way he could be drunk. "What are you talking about?"

"My wife said she watched you give Charlie Parker a tonsillectomy today in the bakery."

"Your wife shouldn't gossip."

"Small town. News travels fast. I'd be surprised if Doc Parker wasn't waiting on the shore with his shotgun when you got back," Cannon added.

"Seriously?" He flipped his collar so it came

high up on his neck then he wiped the sweat from his brow. "It's like living in a fishbowl here." Trig sucked in his cheeks and moved his lips like he was a trout.

"Yep," Bowie said, "but it's the kind of fishbowl where everyone around here feeds you and cleans your water."

"Fair enough. Charlie and I kind of hit it off. She's a good woman, and I like her."

The brothers smiled. "As in like her enough to pursue something?"

Trig rubbed his leg and sat back in one of the chairs Bowie had brought. "I'm keeping my options open." Just then, his line twitched and Trig stood to give it a yank, but the pain in his leg had him falling to the ice and his pole slipped from his hands. Whatever he caught wasn't happy and took off like it was on fire. Even though the Bishop brothers dove for the pole, they couldn't get to it before it disappeared under the ice.

"Some outdoorsmen you are," Bowie teased. "How in the hell am I supposed to feel comfortable offering you a partnership if you can't hold your liquor or your pole?"

Trig wrestled himself up from the cold, hard surface and stood above the hole in the ice. "I'm off my game." He plopped down in the chair and pulled his trouser leg up to look at the scrape on his leg. "I have a little sore spot." That was an understatement, but he didn't want to worry his friends. How was he supposed to be treated like a normal guy when he pointed out his differences?

He reached for his backpack and took out the salve he had. He also took three ibuprofens and opened another beer.

"You okay?" Bowie stood above him, looking at the tender red area.

"Yeah, I'm fine. It's a little cut." He held up the tube of antibiotic ointment. "This will take care of it." The fact that it had in the past made Trig worry less, although, he'd never had an irritation turn this nasty. "Tell me about this partnership."

Cannon, who had already given him a heads' up, lit a Sterno can and pulled out the dogs and buns. In the distance, Trig could see tiny fires like theirs dotting the surface of the frozen lake. At least they weren't the only idiots sitting out in a winter ice storm bonding.

"I'd like to expand the bait and tackle shop to include winter sports like snowshoeing and cross-country skiing, sledding, and snowmobiling. That kind of stuff. In the summer we can offer rowboats and jet skis. There's an outfit across the lake, but the owner is an asshole."

Cannon broke in. "He's an asshole because he tried to hit on Katie early on in their dating."

Bowie chuckled. "There is that, but in all fairness, we weren't actually dating. Hell, we were practically married before we started dating. Sometimes you just know."

"You knew right away?" The subject of insta-love fascinated Trig. He'd never considered Bowie the type. He had always been a hard, gruff man, and yet the guy sitting in front of him had softened. Trig saw the way Bowie looked at his wife and daughter. Would he ever be able to have that?

Bowie pulled in his line and saw the hook was empty, so he baited it up and tossed it back into the slushy water. "My heart knew, but my head was firmly set on staying single. Love is risky and can be painful."

"But is it worth it?" Trig asked.

In the dark, Bowie's smile was like a beacon of light. "Have you seen my daughter? My wife? Need I say more?"

In the distance, a shadow moved toward them. It got bigger as it got closer until a large man stood in front of them carrying a foil-covered tray.

"Did someone order pot roast and potatoes?"

While he hadn't met Dalton Black yet, he'd

heard enough about him to know that the big guy standing in front of them was Aspen Cove's resident chef. Another clue could have been the steam escaping the foil or the rich smell of garlic and brown gravy.

"We were just getting ready to eat dogs."

Dalton looked down at his hands. "I can leave if you'd rather eat almost-cooked wieners and ice cold buns."

"Screw that." Trig hopped up and offered his seat to Dalton.

Dalton turned around to show the portable chair strapped to his back. "I came prepared."

"You staying the night?" Cannon asked as he took the pan from Dalton's hands and peeled off the foil to unveil pot roast, potatoes, and carrots smothered in thick gravy.

Dalton shook his head slowly. "Learned my lesson last time. Happy to dine with friends, but I'm crawling between the sheets with my woman."

They all stared back at the shore and sighed.

"Wimp," Bowie said. "This is a bonding experience. Real he-man shit. You've gotten soft on the love songs Samantha sings you."

Dalton laughed. "Dude, when she sings, I can guarantee you I'm never soft."

Cannon handed out the paper plates he had

tucked inside his backpack. They all dug in. "This is Trig, by the way. Bowie was just negotiating a partnership of sorts."

Dalton nodded his head. "I think expanding is important."

They talked about the culinary school and how most of his business came from the ready-made meals he sold at the end of class. "The fire department can keep me in business all on their own."

Trig sat back and listened to the men talk about how the town had grown over the last year. He envied the way they all seemed to belong to something or someone. He wanted that for himself. He wanted to be a part of something more than him and the sum of his parts.

That's what he'd loved about the military. The camaraderie was amazing, but so was knowing what the mission was and having a solid plan to accomplish it. He'd been floating in uncertainty for far too long. Maybe there was a place for him in Aspen Cove. Maybe if he were lucky, Charlie would find her place here too. If he pushed the odds, maybe they'd be right for each other.

He looked across the lake to the deck of the bed and breakfast. He caught a glimpse of movement and wondered if it was her out there thinking about him.

"If you're serious, I'd be interested. I've got some money put away I can invest, but I have one caveat."

Bowie looked at him. "What's your deal breaker?"

Leave it to his old sergeant to cut through the crap. "You have to treat me like you'd treat any other partner." Trig looked down at his knees. "I don't want any special treatment."

Bowie laughed. "You're getting all the shit I don't want like snowshoeing. I don't give a shit if you have to hop on one foot and crutches to get through it. That's too damn much work for me."

They shook on the deal. Trig hadn't felt that empowered in a long time. Once again, he had a mission and a goal. A few goals, if he added Charlie into the mix.

He brushed the dripping sweat from his forehead. All the while his body shook like a junkie. He also hadn't felt this bad in a long time.

The last thing he heard was Bowie's voice echoing in his head, "Are you all right? Trig, talk to me, man."

CHAPTER TWELVE

Charlie had finished decorating the last of the sugar cookies with Sage when a commotion came from the back deck.

"Call your father," was all Bowie said as he, Cannon, and Dalton stumbled through the back door carrying Trig. Her heart sunk to her bare feet. He was still and pale.

"What the hell happened?" Charlie said as she rushed ahead of them to open Trig's bedroom door. She tossed the clothes he had on the bed away and pulled down the covers.

"Call your dad," Bowie said again. There was more than concern in his expression. He looked downright scared.

Sage walked in and tossed Charlie her

phone. "I called Lydia, she was at Louise's. Looks like the weather isn't only bringing us an ice storm, but also a baby. Louise is stable and Lydia is on her way, too."

Charlie dialed her dad's number. "Daddy, it's Trig, he's not conscious." She brushed her hand to his forehead. "He's got a fever. I need you to come right away." She hung up the phone and started to strip Trig down. "Help me get him out of these clothes. He's burning up."

At any other time it would have been funny to see the faces of three grown men look appalled at stripping a man naked, but Bowie, Cannon, and Dalton were pale with worry.

Medicine was medicine, and Charlie went straight into caregiver mode. She couldn't grow up with a doctor as a father and not glean something from the experience.

When she had Trig in nothing but a sock and boxers, she told Dalton to get a washcloth and a pan of cool water.

She sat on the edge of the bed and mopped at his sweaty brow. He moaned and opened his eyes. "Don't let them take me to the hospital. Please," he begged and closed his eyes again.

Her father rushed inside ten minutes later. "Sorry it took so long. The roads are awful. Covered with ice." He shuffled everyone but Charlie out the door. When Lydia walked inside, Charlie stood back and let them have the space they needed to help Trig.

She was awestruck to watch them work in tandem as if they'd been doing it for years, but seeing her father care for someone she loved brought back old, ugly memories. Anxiety threaded up her spine until it nearly paralyzed her.

"Hundred and four. Blood pressure is elevated at 150/90. Pulse is accelerated." Lydia pulled a stethoscope from her bag and listened to Trig's heart while Charlie's father took a look at his leg.

"He's got a mean infection brewing here. We should call 911 and get him transported to Copper Creek."

"Not going to happen," Lydia said. "I just heard they closed the pass between here and Copper Creek. Silver Springs is impossible to get to as well. No birds are flying. He's not going anywhere."

"No," Charlie cried. While she knew Trig didn't want to go to the hospital, she saw the look on her father's face—the same look he'd had the day her mother died. "He didn't want to go to the hospital, but he needs better care." Her father's soft blue eyes dulled with understanding. She hated that she'd hurt his feelings, but she knew if Trig died, she'd always wonder if was due to his level of care.

Lydia stood back and watched them.

Doc walked to Charlie and set his hands on her shoulders. "Honey, he's a very sick man. He's got an infection." Doc pulled her over to see the festering wound at his amputation site. "He needs antibiotics and an IV and round the clock observation. I have to be honest—"

"No," she said with determination. She looked back at the man she'd come to care for. "You have to leave. Lydia will take care of him."

She could see the wheels turning in her father's head. "Honey, he's going to need round the clock care. I want to be here for you—for him."

"No." Tears ran down her cheeks. "Dad, please go. Go help Louise." She looked at the man covered in scars. "I can't lose you both in the same night."

Her father's features softened and he pulled her to his chest for a big comforting hug.

"You'll have to keep an eye on him."

"Yes, I'll sleep with him." She hadn't meant it that way, but knew her father didn't like hearing that from his daughter.

"Just be with him. I'll get what we need from the clinic and be right back. Lydia and Sage can pull shifts. We can get one of the EMTs here if needed." Doc left.

Lydia gave Charlie a hard look. "You want to tell me what that's about? You just made the man most qualified to care for Trig leave."

Charlie shook her head. "I'd never forgive him if Trig died."

Lydia moved around Trig, checking his vitals again. "Is this about your mother?"

Charlie's head fell. "He should have saved her."

Lydia pulled her to the corner of the room. "I've seen her chart. There was nothing your father could have done."

"You're wrong." She swiped at the tears pooling in her eyes. "He was late getting home. He always took care of everyone else, but when it came to his wife, he wasn't there. I'd upset her an hour before. I caused the stress and he failed to save her."

Lydia frowned. "I don't want to be harsh given the situation, but I feel it's important to be honest." She looked toward Trig. "Your mother was dead before she hit the ground. Her brain bleed was inoperable. Even if an entire team of neurosurgeons had been present they couldn't have saved her. You didn't cause it either. These things can lie dormant for years like a volcano and then erupt."

Charlie stared at Lydia, who had returned to Trig. His body shook from fever. She pressed the cold compress to his forehead.

"He could have told me. He never told me those things."

Lydia shook her head. "Would you have listened? Would you have heard? We'll pull shifts until we know he's out of danger. I'll take the first shift. My sister can take tomorrow."

Charlie threw herself at Lydia. Tears rushed down her cheeks. "I swear I'll make it up to you."

"Don't make it up to me. Make it up to your father. Forgive him. Forgive yourself."

When Doc returned, Charlie sank into the seat in the corner of the room and watched them turn Trig's room into a medical center. Within seconds, he was hooked up to an IV drip that infused his body with antibiotics. A small machine sat on the nightstand monitoring his vitals. When Lydia set out to clean the wound, Trig moaned in pain. Charlie rushed to his side and held his hand. Though he didn't open his eyes, she knew he felt her presence by the way he held onto her as if she tethered him to earth.

The next time Charlie looked up, her father

was gone. Had she made the wrong choice by asking him to leave?

Sage popped in to offer coffee and told her sister that she could monitor him overnight. She was a nurse and fully qualified. No one could argue that fact, so once Trig appeared stable they left Charlie alone with him with strict orders to get Sage if anything seemed off.

She climbed into the bed beside him. "You silly man. You should have told me how badly you hurt yourself."

She touched his forehead and a sense of relief overwhelmed her when he no longer felt on fire. Her fingers skimmed the chiseled plains of his cheekbones and brushed over his soft supple lips. She rose and pressed her mouth to his. "You have to get better. You owe me more kisses."

She waited for his reply, but it never came. She snuggled into the side of his body and draped her hand over his chest. So many scars. So much hurt in his lifetime. While his scars were visible, hers were hidden deep inside her heart.

She woke several hours later when Sage entered the room to change Trig's IV and check his fluid output. She'd winced when they put a catheter in him, but she was grateful that Sage thought it all looked good. While Trig still had a fever, it wasn't as high as before.

"You think he'll be okay?"

Sage frowned. "Infections are dangerous. Right now he seems to be fighting it." She pulled the sheet up to his chest. "You should get some rest. He'll be okay for now."

"No," Charlie replied. "I'm staying with him."

Sage smiled. "He's lucky to have you. Many women wouldn't be able to look past all this. Especially since you've only just met."

Charlie sat on the edge of the bed and brought Trig's hand into her lap. "As crazy as it sounds, I feel like I've known him forever."

Sage turned and walked to the door. "Like I said, he's lucky to have you."

Charlie gave her a weak smile. "Somehow I think I'm the lucky one."

Sage told her she'd check on him in a few hours. She shut the light off and closed the doors.

"Don't you die on me, Trig Whatley. I have plans for you." She snuggled into his side and fell asleep.

The next morning Clovis nudged her awake. Dogs always had that funny sixth sense and Clovis had somehow known Trig was ill.

The door opened and Lydia walked inside.

"I'll take it from here. Go get some coffee and something to eat. Agatha dropped off Bisquick breakfast casserole."

At the mention of Agatha, Charlie felt the waves of guilt flood her senses. She'd come to Aspen Cove to make amends with her father and yet she'd basically shut him out of her life again. She didn't want to leave the room and face her truth. She'd been unreasonable. Unfair. Her actions had been unwarranted. "I want to stay." She wiped the sleep from her eyes.

"The last thing he needs is for you to get sick too. I promise he'll be fine while you fortify."

Charlie leaned over and pressed a kiss to Trig's cheek. "Get better fast," she told him. "Tomorrow's Christmas." She turned to Lydia. "Is it normal for him to sleep so long?"

Lydia walked her to the door. "Sleep is the best thing he can get. It can't hurt you either."

Charlie knew she was right, but she also knew in her heart that it would mean a lot to Trig if she was there when he woke up. Lord how she wanted—no—she needed him to wake up.

When she walked into the living room she was met with her father, who sat on the couch staring out the window at the frozen lake.

"Dad, what are you doing here?"

Dark circles sat like coal smudges under his

tired eyes. "Did you think I'd leave and not come back? I refuse to disappoint you again. Even if you don't want me to provide care for that man, the least I can do is provide support for you."

Charlie rushed to her father and fell into his arms. The last time he'd held her while she cried was the night her mother died. How could she forget that while he grieved the loss of his one great love, he still nurtured her?

"I'm so sorry. I know it wasn't your fault."

He thumbed her tears from her cheeks. "Oh honey, I would have saved her if I could. I would have given her my life if possible. It wasn't possible. There was nothing I could do."

Charlie sat back and really looked at her father for the first time in a decade. She'd missed him so much. "Daddy," she said in a small voice. "Trig needs you."

Though her father was visibly exhausted, his broad smile made him seem recharged.

"You want me to help Lydia?"

Charlie shook her head. "No."

Doc gave her a confused look. "Okay, honey. Whatever you want."

"Lydia can assist you in making sure Trig recovers. He needs the best care and that will always be you. I'm sorry I forgot about who you were for a second. You're Doc Parker and you're like a wizard in these parts. Go work your magic." She moved off her father's lap and helped him to his feet.

"I'll do my best, sweetheart."

She hugged him hard. "That's all I can ask for." She gave him a hug. "How's Louise?"

Doc smiled, "Aspen Cove has a new resident. Paul Robert Williams was born at three o'clock this morning."

"She named him after you?"

Her father smiled with pride. "It's about time. I've delivered every single one of those kids."

"I'm so happy she honored you." She felt a stab of guilt for not showing him the same respect the last ten years.

While her father went to care for Trig, Charlie entered the kitchen to grab a plate of breakfast casserole and visit with everyone that had congregated there. It was as if the entire town was holding vigil over Trig. In reality, it was only the Bishops, Dalton and Samantha, Wes, and Agatha who were present. Of course, Sage was there too since it was her bed and breakfast. The kitchen counters were filled with foil-covered dishes and plates of muffins from Katie.

"Where did all this stuff come from?"

Charlie lifted a muffin from the plate and took a bite.

"You know what small town life is like," Dalton said. "Word gets out and people cook, it's what they do."

Charlie's father came out of Trig's room looking relaxed. "He's still asleep." He walked over to Agatha and gave her a kiss. It warmed Charlie's heart that he'd found love in his seventies. Kind of made her jealous that at twenty-eight, she'd never found it at all until she picked up a man and his dog on the side of the road.

"I'll be right back." She rushed into the living room where she found the basset hound curled up next to Otis. She dropped to the floor and pulled him into her lap. After a few wet sloppy kisses, he let her look at his eye. When she saw that the eye was healing nicely, she let out a whoop of excitement. A few more doses of antibiotic ointment and the dog would be good as new.

As the morning turned into the afternoon and then the evening, Charlie traded places with her father, Lydia, and Sage as they took turns caring for Trig. The more time she spent alone with him, the more she came to appreciate who he was as a man. She'd nearly memorized every scar on his body. She'd certainly memorized the feel of his lips from the kisses she stole every few minutes. While her father changed his IV bag, Charlie walked outside and sat on the same chair where she'd curled into Trig's lap days ago. Had it only been a few days?

She stared into the clear night sky and gazed at the thousands of sparking stars. She found the brightest one and closed her eyes in prayer.

As a child, every Christmas Eve, Charlie headed outside with her mother and they wished upon the brightest star. Phyllis Parker called it the Christmas Eve Star and told Charlie that if she wanted something bad enough, the Christmas Eve angels would do their best to grant the wish. She hadn't wished on that star in ten years. In her mind, the angels owed her.

"Please heal Trig," she whispered. While she'd like to say the prayer wasn't for her but an unselfish hope to heal a stranger, she knew she wanted him healthy as much for herself as she did for him. She wanted it for her father too, because even if she wouldn't hold him responsible if Trig didn't heal, she knew her father would never forgive himself.

"Sweetheart," her father said from behind her. "Agatha and I are heading out. We'll be by in the morning. He's sleeping peacefully. His fever has broken and his wound is healing."

Charlie hugged her father hard. "Dad, thanks for everything. I have a feeling everything is going to be okay."

He kissed her forehead. "You know what, Charlie? I think you're right."

She stayed on the deck for a few more minutes before she went back to Trig's room and climbed into his bed. She giggled at the fact that she'd already slept with him, and he had no idea. As soon as he was better, she'd make sure the next time she spent the night tucked next to his body he'd remember it.

CHAPTER THIRTEEN

Trig woke to the beeping of machines. He felt the telltale tug of an IV line in his arm. While his right side was cool, his left side was hot and heavy.

A body moved next to him. He didn't have to see her to know it was Charlie. She smelled like cinnamon and sugar—like toaster pastries or maple syrup. She smelled like happiness.

The last thing he remembered was sitting on the ice with the guys. He had a vague recollection of being put into a bed.

He shifted and she flew up from a sound sleep. "Are you okay?" She rubbed at her eyes, which were rimmed in deep shadows.

"I'm perfect. Where are we?" He tried to lift up, but she pushed him back down.

"Don't move," she said.

She grabbed her phone and called her father while Trig took in the situation around him. He was still in his room at the bed and breakfast.

"What happened?"

Charlie tried to move off the bed, but he pulled her back to his side.

"I got my wish. That's what happened. I asked for you to get healthy and to wake up and look at you."

He pieced together the bits that he knew. "You didn't let them take me to the hospital." He leaned into her and kissed her lips.

"You begged me not to but I would have if it meant saving you. However, there was an ice storm."

"Give me a kiss."

"How can I deny a begging man?"

"You like me." He knew his smile was broad because he saw its reflection in her eyes. Eyes that looked tired with worry but happy with relief.

"I more than like you, mister. While you were sleeping I decided I could love you."

"Is that right?"

She nodded. "Of course, that means we'd

have to spend more time together because I need you to learn to love me too."

He chuckled. "Charlie, look at me. I'm a mess and you want to love me?"

She brushed back his hair and peppered his face with kisses. "Too late. I think I already do."

"It's settled then. I will love you forever, too," he said.

She scooted close to him. "You'll have to because we've slept together and my father knows. I told him to bring his shotgun."

"You slept with me last night?"

"The last two nights. It's Christmas, silly. Merry Christmas, Trig Whatley. I've got nothing to give you but my heart."

It was hard to maneuver with the IV, but he managed to roll on his side and wrap her in his arms. "You've given me so much already. You've given me hope. Now kiss me," he repeated. "I miss your kisses."

She laughed. "There's so much you missed while you were sleeping."

"Tell me."

"I've given you at least a hundred Christmas kisses." Just as he was getting his one hundred and first, Doc Parker walked into the room and cleared his throat.

"Good morning, Trig. Merry Christmas."

Trig sat up, but didn't let Charlie escape from his side. "Good morning, sir. Merry Christmas."

Doc took his vitals and deemed he was going to be all right. When he asked Charlie to leave so he could remove the catheter and IV, she laughed. "I've seen it all, Daddy. Trig isn't hiding anything from me."

Doc gave them both a dark look. "Son, when you're feeling better, you and I are going to have to have a talk about your intentions toward my daughter."

Trig gave Charlie's hand a squeeze before he asked her to step out of the room.

Doc removed everything that kept Trig tied to the bed.

"Sir, I think I love your daughter. My intentions are as follows. Number one, I plan on buying us a house and staying here in Aspen Cove where I'll partner with Bowie and provide for your daughter. Number two, I plan on marrying her as soon as she'll say yes. Number three, I plan on making her the happiest woman in the world. If you give me your blessings, I'll get to work on it right away."

Doc sat at the edge of the bed and looked Trig straight in the eye. "Son, if you're not feeling too weak, get yourself dressed and meet me in the living room." He pointed to a pair of crutches in the corner. "Use those until your leg heals a few more days."

Trig wasn't sure if meeting him in the living room was a good thing or not. That certainly put him closer to the front door. Was Doc getting ready to boot him to the curb?

"Should I be worried?"

"Only if you don't make her happy. I may be old, but I'm determined." Doc rose from the bed and walked to the door. "I'd ask if you needed help, but you're the stubborn type. Just don't fall and break your head. She'd never forgive me."

Trig swung his leg over the edge and stood up slowly. Lucky for him he'd had plenty of fluids the last few days so he wasn't particularly dizzy or unstable. His stomach growled, telling him he was hungry. He hopped to the bathroom, took a quick shower, dressed, and hobbled his way into the living room, where Doc and Agatha sat on the sofa together. Cannon and Sage sat cross-legged in front of the tree. Clovis and Otis were spooned in the dog bed.

Charlie came out of the kitchen with two cups of coffee. "I thought you might like some more liquid." Trig made his way to an empty chair and as soon as Charlie set the cups down, he pulled her into his lap. She squealed with delight.

"Merry Christmas," he said to everyone present. "I'm sorry to put a damper on the holidays."

Charlie smiled. "You didn't. You helped us see it's not what you have, but who you have that matters. Christmas is about family and friends."

Doc rose from his seat and walked a plain white box to Charlie. "I've been holding on to these for years hoping that someday you would find it in your heart to come home." He handed her the box.

Trig swiped the tear that ran down her cheek.

Charlie cleared her throat. "You know what's so funny about that statement? I had to come home to find my heart." She opened the box and inside was two keys. "Really?"

Trig had no idea what that meant, so he looked between father and daughter.

"They have always been yours. Your mother would have wanted you to have the house and the space next to the clinic has been waiting for you since the day you left."

She turned to him. "I've got a house and a clinic. Now all I need is a partner. What do you say, Trig Whatley? You want to take a chance on me?"

He turned toward Doc Parker.

"Son, I took care of number one on your list. It's up to you to take care of the rest."

He would have liked to get up and shake on the deal, but that would require letting go of Charlie. In his heart, it was too great a sacrifice. He knew he'd never let her go, not even for a moment.

Trig spent the rest of the Christmas day enjoying his new family. When the sun set, he feigned exhaustion and led Charlie to his room which Sage had turned back into his very own romantic getaway with wine for Charlie and candles for ambience. While Doc warned him not to exert himself, there was no way he wasn't making love to her. He didn't care that his body was recovering. Nothing mattered except Charlie and making her realize she was his for all time and eternity.

"So you saw it all, huh?" He tossed his crutches to the side and pulled his T-shirt over his chest. His hands skimmed over the countless scars running across his skin. "Everything?"

He tugged at the button of his jeans and pulled the zipper down one tooth at a time.

She blushed, but her eyes never left him. She

didn't look at him in horror, but in awe. He watched as her chest rose and fell and her breath picked up.

"Everything. How could I not? You're so perfect."

"You're so blind." He bent his finger and motioned for her to join him. She didn't hesitate. "Charlie, I'm going to make love to you tonight. You belong to me. You belong with me. I know it's quick but..."

She placed her fingers over his lips. "Stop talking and do it."

Trig wasted no time getting her naked. She lay in the center of the mattress. Her soft white skin glowed against the blue sheets. He climbed on top of the bed resting on both knees and, while his left was painfully sore, nothing would be more painful than not making love to her.

He brushed his lips against hers and trailed down the column of her neck to her shoulders and then to her perfect breasts. As he plucked a pebbled nipple into his mouth, the only thing he felt was alive.

He made love to her breasts, making sure to spend equal time between them before he moved south. His tongue ran down her stomach until he dipped inside her belly button. And when he came to the sweet spot between her thighs, he loved her for long minutes. When she shook and shuddered beneath his tongue with a whisper of his name on her lips he knew he'd be hers forever.

He shifted up her body. His erection lay painfully heavy between his legs. "Would you be unhappy if you got pregnant our first time?"

She stalled for a second and then gripped his hips and pulled him deep inside her. "Haven't we wasted enough time?"

He stilled inside, knowing he'd never felt this good in all his life. Here was a woman who knew he was lacking and yet she made him feel whole.

He thrust forward and pulled back until her breath caught in her throat and his name left her lips again. The flutter of her release pulled him deeper until he sailed over the edge with her.

They lay in each other's arms. "How did you know I was the one?" she asked.

He laughed. "You told me with every kiss. While I might not have known in my head, I knew in my heart."

CHAPTER FOURTEEN
TWO MONTHS LATER

She stood back and looked at the fireplace mantel. Front and center was her wedding photo. She'd worn her mother's simple white dress while her father married them. Trig was so damn handsome in his suit and tie. While it might be odd to some to marry at the cemetery, Charlie wanted her mother present. She knew she was there when way ahead of the season a single yellow crocus bloomed on her grave.

Everyone joked about a shotgun wedding, but they would have married regardless of the fact that Charlie was eight weeks pregnant. A girl couldn't go wrong with a wounded warrior who loved basset hounds.

"Is that everything you wanted from your

dad's?" Trig walked over to her and laid his hand on her flat stomach.

"I've got you. What else do I need?"

"You keep telling yourself that. Just remember when it comes to marrying me there are no refunds or returns. I come as is."

She lifted and kissed him. They'd spent the first month together getting the vet clinic set up. Not only had her father saved the building for her, but he'd also saved her mother's life insurance policy to make sure it was state of the art.

It was the best day ever when she walked into her old job to pick up her check and introduce her fiancé to good ole Evan Barkman.

They also stopped to see Trig's mom and dad. He wasn't keen on visiting his parents, but Charlie thought it important they meet her before the couple married.

Somehow, the sight of their son with a woman who loved him changed the way his parents saw him. Now that he'd made a fresh start, including a new business venture and a successful fiancé who adored him, they saw him as the strong young man they had raised, not the crippled war vet who came back to them. When they got the seal of approval, they headed home only to find out that Charlie was indeed pregnant.

"When are you going to show?"

She laughed. "What is it about you? First you have an overweight dog, and now you want to have an overweight wife."

He picked her up and carried her to the bedroom. "I can't wait until you're big with my baby."

The one thing she hadn't told Trig yet was she was bound to get really big because that first night he made love to her at the bed and breakfast, the angels blessed them twice. "What if I get huge? I mean really huge? Will you love me then?"

He pulled her shirt up and kissed her stomach. "I'll love you twice as much."

"Oh good, because honey...we're having twins."

Next up is One Hundred Lifetimes

OTHER BOOKS BY KELLY COLLINS

An Aspen Cove Romance Series

One Hundred Reasons

One Hundred Heartbeats

One Hundred Wishes

One Hundred Promises

One Hundred Excuses

One Hundred Christmas Kisses

One Hundred Lifetimes

One Hundred Ways

One Hundred Goodbyes

One Hundred Secrets

One Hundred Regrets

One Hundred Choices

One Hundred Decisions

One Hundred Glances

One Hundred Lessons

One Hundred Mistakes

One Hundred Nights

One Hundred Whispers
One Hundred Reflections
One Hundred Intentions
One Hundred Chances
One Hundred Dreams

GET A FREE BOOK.

Go to www.authorkellycollins.com

ABOUT THE AUTHOR

International bestselling author of more than thirty novels, Kelly Collins writes with the intention of keeping love alive. Always a romantic, she blends real-life events with her vivid imagination to create characters and stories that lovers of contemporary romance, new adult, and romantic suspense will return to again and again.

For More Information
www.authorkellycollins.com
kelly@authorkellycollins.com

Made in the USA
Monee, IL
27 May 2023